"Trap you? I wouldn't
be seen dead with you!"

Sophie flung her words defiantly
against Alex's accusation. Suddenly
she heard the intake of his breath, felt
him tense. Then his arms closed
around her in savage possession. He
forced her head back under the
pressure of his kiss, exploring her
open mouth in a probing invasion she
could not escape. She backed away
struggling as he advanced, crushing
her against the window, pulsing with
desire she could feel in her own body.

"That's the game, isn't it?" Alex
ground out. "You can't marry Simon,
so you cold-bloodedly planned to
trap me. It might have worked if I
hadn't been lucky enough to see the
two of you together!"

"You're wrong!" Sophie gasped. But
somehow she knew she would not be
spared Alex's anger—nor his
ridiculous idea of revenge!

Other titles by

CHARLOTTE LAMB
IN HARLEQUIN PRESENTS

Other titles by

CHARLOTTE LAMB
IN HARLEQUIN ROMANCES

CHARLOTTE LAMB

savage surrender

Harlequin Books

TORONTO • LONDON • LOS ANGELES • AMSTERDAM
SYDNEY • HAMBURG • PARIS • STOCKHOLM • ATHENS • TOKYO

Harlequin Presents edition published December 1980
ISBN 0-373-10401-4

Original hardcover edition published in 1980
by Mills & Boon Limited

CHAPTER ONE

AUTUMN was passing into a melancholy winter, the London trees stripped now and skeletal against the rainy sky, the gutters filled with sodden leaves which were slowly reducing to thin grey lace. The streets around Liverpool Street Station were grey and wet, filled with hurrying figures. Taxis poured up from inside the station. The roads were jammed with traffic.

Sophie looked up at the leaden skies and thought of the winter ahead with gloom, longing for blue skies and sunshine. Already she felt as if it was years since she had seen the sun, and it was only November. She paused outside a travel agency to stare at a gaudy poster, sighing.

The rain thickened and she began to hurry, head bent, knowing her route so well after the two years she had spent working at the Lefkas Shipping Office in the Minories that she did not even look up as she walked.

As she came towards the office, a sleek white limousine drew up outside it and a woman stepped out, an umbrella held over her head by an attentive chauffeur in a peaked cap and dark uniform. Sophie was unaware of them, still hurrying. The man stepped backwards suddenly and sent her flying. She might not have fallen if the pavements had not been wet and slippery, but her foot skidded as she tried to retrieve her balance and she fell heavily.

'Well, help her, help her,' the woman exclaimed in thickly accented English. 'Don't just stand there, man!'

The chauffeur had hesitated, but now he moved towards Sophie, his employer having snatched the umbrella from his hand. Sophie was already struggling to her feet as he reached her. Wet mud streaked hands, knees and face, her raincoat had a long smear running across the front of it and her stockings were torn.

'All right, miss?' The chauffeur ineffectually brushed at her coat and Sophie gave him a dry look.

'I can manage, thank you.' She glanced round for her umbrella, furious to see it spinning off into the busy road. A second later a car passed over it with a squeal of brakes, then righted itself to go on, the driver looking round with a scowl. 'Oh, no!' Sophie muttered through her teeth. Her umbrella flapped wetly in the middle of the road, the spokes broken, a pathetic object now.

'Come under here, child,' the woman said, extending her own umbrella to cover Sophie's head. Brought close to her, Sophie recognised her and a look of surprise crossed her face.

'Oh! Madame!' she said involuntarily, and the woman gave her a quick look and smiled.

'You work for us? Of course you do. Come along, we must get you tidied up. You look as if you have been in an accident.'

Madame Lefkas had taken her arm and was urging her through the swing doors and into the elevator before Sophie had had time to think. Turning to her chauffeur, Madame said: 'Brown, take her coat back to the flat and get Vinny to press it and clean it at once. Tell Vinny to give you some nylons too.' Giving Sophie a measuring glance, she added thoughtfully: 'I think mine should fit her.'

Sophie protested, flushing: 'There's no need...'

'Nonsense. The accident was our fault. Brown knocked you down.'

The chauffeur looked wooden.

'Take off your coat, child,' said Madame, waving an imperious hand at her.

'Really—' Sophie began, but Madame said firmly: 'Ssh, ssh!' Leaning forward, she undid Sophie's top button and Sophie automatically completed the job. As she slid out of the coat the chauffeur took it over his arm. He stayed in the elevator to go down again while Madame guided Sophie out into the carpeted reception area on the top floor which housed the chairman's suite of offices.

The receptionist rose to her feet, a smile on her well-groomed face. 'Coffee, my dear,' said Madame. 'For two in the chairman's office in five minutes.' Passing the staring girl, Sophie was steered very firmly into the chairman's office, where Madame gestured to a door. 'You can wash in the bathroom.'

Sophie thanked her rather uncertainly and went into the room. It took her some time to wash her face, remove her torn pantyhose and wash her grazed knees.

She carefully combed her thick fair hair, renewed her make-up and inspected herself before going out to Madame. Seated on a long cream couch with a coffee table in front of her, Madame beckoned. 'Come and sit down, child.'

'I really should get down to my office. I shall be late.' Sophie hesitated in front of her, a frown on her forehead.

'Where do you work?'

'I'm Mr Harrison's secretary.'

There was a knock at the door and Madame called, 'Come,' looking round as the chauffeur stepped into the room with a small cardboard box.

'Ah, the hose,' said Madame, smiling. 'Brown, tell that girl out there to let Mr Harrison know that his secretary is with me.'

Brown nodded, presenting her with the box.

When he had gone Madame handed it to Sophie. Opening it doubtfully, Sophie found it filled with unopened packets of stockings. She took a packet out and put the box down. 'Thank you. You're very kind.'

'Run and put them on,' Madame ordered. 'Do you like cream in your coffee? Sugar?'

'Cream, no sugar,' Sophie agreed, rising.

When she came back Madame gave her a vivid smile which told Sophie how beautiful she must have been when she was young. Her face was thin and lined now, her skin sallow under her make-up, her dark eyes large and very bright.

'Now, what is your name?' she asked Sophie.

'Sophie Bryant.'

'Sophie? Did you know that that is one of the most popular Greek names? Only in Greece it is Sophia.'

'I did know,' Sophie admitted. 'I was named for my grandmother, who was Greek.'

Madame Lefkas looked interested, smiling. 'So? Have you been to Greece?'

'Several times,' Sophie told her. 'I wish I was there now.' She glanced wryly at the rain-wet window. 'London in winter is very depressing.'

Madame laughed. 'Do you speak Greek, Sophie?'

'A little. When I was small, my grandmother talked to me in her own language and I've tried to keep it up since she died. I can read it quite well, but I expect my accent is appalling.'

Madame broke into Greek, speaking slowly, and Sophie laughed as she answered.

'Which part of Greece have you visited?'

'Athens and the Peloponnese, Corfu and Crete, but next year I hope I shall be able to tour the Cyclades.'

'You have been to Crete?' Madame watched her as she asked, still speaking Greek.

'Only for two days.'

'Did you like it?'

Sophie's green eyes shimmered with excitement. 'Of

course. Who wouldn't?'

'I live there, did you know?'

'I knew you lived in Greece, of course,' Sophie nodded, speaking slowly because she found it difficult to translate English into Greek.

'Drink your coffee, child,' said Madame, her dark eyes intent on Sophie's excited face.

Sophie picked up her cup and sipped it.

'Your hair is a most unusual colour,' Madame went on, reverting to English. 'What we in Greece call golden fire, fair hair with a tinge of red in it, the colour which Carpaccio and Tintoretto loved.' She shot Sophie a quick glance. 'Do you like paintings?'

Half laughing, half surprised, Sophie nodded. 'I almost went to art school, but I decided I wasn't good enough.'

'You decided?' Madame enquired drily. 'Not your teachers?'

'They urged me to go,' Sophie shrugged. 'But I felt that although I was good enough perhaps to earn a living when I left art school, I wasn't good enough to be as good as I would want to be—so I took a secretarial course instead. I have a younger sister who's very clever and I knew my parents would find it hard to support both of us through a long training.'

'What is your sister doing now?'

'She's still at university,' Sophie told her. 'Patsy is very bright. She wants to be a doctor.'

Having finished her coffee she put her cup down and gave Madame a polite smile. 'Thank you for being so kind. I think I should get back to work now.'

'Perhaps,' said Madame, watching her. 'We have a large office in Athens, you know. Have you ever thought of working there?'

Laughing, Sophie said: 'Often. I'd love to live in

Greece and I'm hoping to be sent to Athens for a year some time.'

Staff could spend a year abroad at one of the various offices of the company, if they wished, and many in fact moved from one foreign posting to another, although few secretaries followed that route. It was generally executives who wanted to work abroad. The female staff changed so frequently and got married before they were eligible for a foreign posting.

'You have no romantic attachment to keep you in England?' Madame asked her. 'No handsome young man waiting to sweep you off your feet?'

Sophie looked at her wryly. 'No.' She rose and murmured another polite thank you and moved to the door.

'Do you believe in fate, Sophie?' Madame asked as she opened it.

Sophie looked back, eyes opening wide. 'I've never thought about it.'

Madame laughed softly. 'Goodbye, Sophie.'

Sophie returned in the elevator to her own floor. Her normally tart boss only gave her a curious smile when she walked into his office. 'How did you come to meet Madame?' She told him and he whistled. Glancing down at her long legs, he grinned. 'Hurt yourself?'

'No,' she said coldly. Sophie did not like Mr Harrison much; he watched her in a way she found unpleasant and he took every opportunity he could to touch her. Married with two children, he was in his early forties, a heavy fleshy man with a smile that was a little false and a voice that held far too much insinuation when he spoke to her. He had once or twice tried to persuade her to have dinner with him. Sophie kept him at a distance but would have liked to move elsewhere if she could. She only put up with him because she liked working for the Lefkas organisation.

Settling back to work, she imagined she would never see Madame again. Although the Lefkas family kept a controlling eye on all the parts of their far-flung empire they only visited London fleetingly, and even then it was usually Madame's son, Alex, who came. Madame spent most of her time in Greece.

A week later Sophie was summoned to the chairman's office again. Her boss walked into her little office and gave her a slightly sneering smile. 'You're wanted upstairs—the chairman himself this time.'

'Mr Lefkas?' Sophie was taken aback, staring at him.

'Moving in exalted circles, aren't we?' Mr Harrison had only met Alex Lefkas himself once or twice and he did not bother to hide his irritation. 'I should get knocked down by Madame's chauffeur. It obviously works a charm!'

Sophie walked to the door, her spine prickling at the way he watched her.

'Lefkas likes blondes,' he said nastily. 'Flash those beautiful legs at him and you'll be set up for life.'

Sophie ignored that, and went out, her skin flushed. Why did Alex Lefkas want to see her? she wondered, going up in the elevator. When she emerged the receptionist gave her a curious smile. 'Go straight in, he's expecting you.'

Surely Alex Lefkas wasn't going to tear a strip off her for talking to his mother? Sophie thought as she opened his door. The whole family were always treated obsequiously by the staff, as though they were royalty, bowed into the building with smiles and flattering eagerness.

She had seen Alex Lefkas at a distance but never been so close to him before. Closing the door, she walked towards his desk and he looked up from the letter he was reading.

She received an impression of sardonic impatience in the quick, all-seeing glance he threw her. He was sitting behind a wide, leather-topped desk which was covered in papers and telephones. A large office console stood at his elbow. A cup of half-drunk coffee stood in front of him. He leaned back in his chair, his black head tilted, laid down the letter and stared at her intently, a restless flicker of speculation in his eyes.

She waited for him to speak, but for a moment he said nothing, the silvery grey eyes flicking from her bright golden head to her feet and taking in the slender elegance of her white silk blouse and charcoal grey skirt.

Sophie became convinced she was about to be fired for presumption. Her green eyes met his defiantly as he looked back at her face.

Waving a hand at the chair placed in front of his desk, he said, 'Sit down, Miss Bryant.' His English was even more fluent than his mother's and had a trace of an American accent running beside the deep harsh tones which came from his native tongue.

Sophie sat down, lifting her head in a graceful movement, her eyes on his face.

'So your grandmother was Greek,' he said abruptly.

Sophie's eyes widened. 'Yes.'

He glanced down at a folder, pulled it towards him and opened it. Bending forward he ran his eye over the first paper inside it and Sophie was able to observe him closely without his being aware of it. His dark striped suit was formally elegant, but he wore it with a casual panache which underplayed the style and cut, the jacket flung open, his silk tie loosened, his collar open at the throat to reveal the strong brown column of his neck.

Leaning back, he surveyed her coolly. 'Helena Sophia Argentopolis,' he said. Sophia stared, her lips parting in surprise.

'Born Corinth on the first day of May 1901, married George Bryant, an official of the Bank of England then resident in Athens in 1920, had three children by him and died in 1970 of pneumonia.' He observed Sophia's dumbfounded face with a twist of his mouth. 'I know everything about you, Miss Bryant, you see.'

Her green eyes gazed at him. She was speechless. What was going on? Surely even the Lefkas organisation did not investigate their employees that closely? Especially an unimportant secretary!

'My mother wants you to come to Crete to work for her,' Alex Lefkas went on, keeping those cool grey eyes fixed on her.

'Work for your mother? Me?' Sophie did not know what she had been expecting—but it hadn't been that, and her look of amazement seemed to amuse him. His dark brows curved upwards mockingly.

'You seem surprised. Had you no suspicion that that was in her mind?'

She shook her head, the light catching it and making the red lights flame among the gold. Alex Lefkas's grey eyes lifted to watch even as he said, 'Well, what do you say? Will you go?' He clearly expected a reply, but it was all so sudden, so unexpected, that Sophie found it difficult to grasp any of the implications. In total confusion, she just stared at him, and his eyes narrowed as though he were impatient with her.

'Come along, Miss Bryant, do you want the job or don't you?'

'You must have an answer now?' Sophie asked hesitantly.

'My mother was under the impression that you wanted to work in Greece. Was she wrong?'

'No,' Sophie said at once. 'No, I do, but I hadn't expected ...'

'Clearly,' he bit out. 'Make up your mind—I don't have all day. I've spent a great deal of time on this business already. I've got more important things on my mind!'

A slight flush came into her face and she gave him a quick, angry glance. 'Yes,' she said.

He put both hands flat on his desk and leaned towards her. 'Does that mean yes, you want the job, or yes, you know I have more important things of my mind?'

'I want the job,' Sophie said coldly.

He studied her without expression. 'I'll leave it to Patros to give you the details. I wanted to take a look at you myself before I decided whether or not you would do. My mother's too softhearted. Don't try to take advantage of her kindness or you'll have me to deal with.'

She looked at him and could believe that. If there was one thing about him that stood out a mile it was that he was definitely not soft-hearted. One glance told you that. In his mid-thirties, a tall man, lean and powerful, the very way he sat in that chair informed you of the driving dynamism which ran the Lefkas empire with hard efficiency. His mother's face had been thin and spare, but his face was toughly modelled, filled with energy and impatience, his cheekbones sharply angular beneath sunbrowned skin which, in his mother, had that lined fragility but which was of the same sallow colouring under the tan. His nose was long and arrogant, his mouth hard and controlled but with a faint, betraying sensuality in the lower lip. His jawline had the faintest trace of shadow along it, closely shaven though he was, but it was the assertive jut of the jaw which impressed on sight.

'We shall want you to fly to Athens at once. Have you a passport?' He watched her as he spoke, his eyes moving over her speculatively.

'Yes,' Sophie nodded.

'How soon can you leave?'

'My work—' she began, but he cut in impatiently.

'Forget your job here. Someone else will take over with Harrison. How soon can you wind up your own personal problems?'

'A few days,' Sophie suggested. She only had to give notice at her apartment, see her family. There was no one in London who would miss her.

Alex Lefkas leaned back in his chair and one long sinewy hand dipped into the pocket of his waistcoat to pull out the gold watch he wore with the fine gilt chain draped across his waist. Glancing at it, he asked without looking at her, 'There are no men in your life. Why?'

Sophie stiffened, not answering.

He shot her a look, his dark brows a straight line across his forehead, his eyes hard and narrowed. 'Well?'

Pulling herself together, she shrugged. 'I haven't got an answer for that.' Not an answer she had any intention of giving Alex Lefkas, anyway, she thought.

His eyes pierced her face as though trying to read whatever lay behind the cool green eyes. After a moment he shrugged his wide shoulders. 'My mother told me you had hair like golden fire. I presume all the fire is in your hair.'

Before Sophie could react to that he picked up the letter he had originally been reading and bent his dark head over it. She sat there, waiting, bemused by his silence.

After a moment he looked up, dark brows arching. 'Well?'

Only then did she understand that she had been summarily dismissed. She got to her feet, feeling an intense dislike for him, and walked to the door. As she opened it she glanced back to say goodbye, but he was intent on what he was reading. She was already forgotten, a detail he had personally attended to because his mother was involved, but someone unimportant, immediately swept out of his thoughts as soon has he had dealt with her.

Over the next few days she felt frequently as though she were in the centre of a storm. She whirled through the days, barely conscious of what was happening, talking to the manager, Mr Patros, arranging to have her possessions sent home to her parents, giving notice at her apartment and packing all her clothes.

Her life in London had been lonely. She found the city lightless and empty, the crowded streets as isolated as a desert island for someone without a family or any close friends.

Several of the men at the shipping office had made advances to her, but she had repulsed them all firmly. She had no interest in going out with any of them. For five years all her attention had been fixed on one man and there was no room in her mind for anyone else.

It was from Mr Patros that she learnt to her incredulity that Alex Lefkas had had her investigated thoroughly before offering her the job. When she stared at him in disbelief, Patros had smiled, his gold-toothed gums revealed briefly. 'Why should you be surprised?'

'But what did he want to know about me?' she asked him, shaking her bright head incredulously. 'What did he think there was to know?'

Shrugging his plump shoulders, his bald head flushed and shining as he relaxed after a long business lunch, Patros said throatily, 'Madame is very, very wealthy. It is Alex's task to protect her from herself, from anyone who might try to milk her of some of that money. She has had employees before now who have tried to cheat her. Alex never leaves anything to chance. You were checked out rigorously.' Giving her another of his smiles, he added, 'Especially where your men friends were concerned. Alex needed to know what sort of woman you were—what sort of men you went around with, if you had any lovers.'

Sophie felt herself colouring hotly. She was horrified, shaken, to realise what sort of world she was entering. Alex Lefkas had had no right to pry into her private life! She said so, and Patros gave a chuckle, spreading his plump ringed hands.

'That is how he is, Miss Bryant. Be warned—Alex Lefkas has an instinct for deception. Don't try to hide anything from him. He is merciless if he thinks he has been cheated.'

Sophie stared at his bland, smiling face and wondered if she was doing the right thing in getting involved with the Lefkas family. She had not anticipated getting enmeshed in the sort of world where every contact, every action, was stringently examined. Of course, she had nothing to fear from any probe, however searching, since she had no ulterior motives in taking the job. She wanted to work in Greece and she would do as good a job as she could. It might be distasteful to know that from now on her whole life would be under a microscope and might at any time be examined by Alex Lefkas's cold hard eyes, but what harm could there be for her in it? Her life was an open book.

Except her thoughts, she told herself drily, and those were surely her own business. Even Alex Lefkas could not demand to be shown the inside of her head.

Could he?

Later she was deeply glad that she had followed her own instincts and gone to Greece. Madame Lefkas was waiting for her in Athens at a large, modern hotel in the centre of the city. She greeted Sophie with delight, surprising her by giving her a kiss on the cheek.

'I am happy you decided to come, child,' she said. 'You are sure you won't get bored working for an old woman in a quiet little villa in Crete?'

'Quite sure,' Sophie said firmly, smiling back at her.

'And there is no heartbroken young man mourning for you in London?' Madame's bright dark eyes questioned her closely as she asked that.

Sophie shook her head, her face sobering.

Madame gave her a wicked grin. 'Perhaps you will meet a handsome Greek while you are here and marry and stay here for good! But not yet, I hope. Let me have a year of your time, child. Patros and Alex will have told you that I want a companion more than a secretary, although you will have secretarial duties to perform for me.'

'They explained,' said Sophie, although it had been Mr Patros who had explained not Alex Lefkas.

'Before we go to Crete we must do some shopping,' Madame announced, glancing at Sophie's neat blue dress and grimacing. 'Alex gave me orders to buy you some new clothes. He rang me to tell me that my new doll, as he called you, was on her way to me, but said he hoped I would do something about your boring clothes or people would think I had bought you from an Oxfam shop.'

Sophie's green eyes flared angrily, and Madame laughed, watching her. 'Ah, that annoys you? Good. Alex is very high-handed, and I need someone around me who can say no to him. All my servants at the villa have known him since he was tiny and he can twist them round his little finger. What bulldozing cannot achieve, Alex tries to get with charm, and he always gets his own way in the end. My last two secretaries fell madly in love with him. It was very irritating—they worked for him, not me. I want someone who will look after my interests, not those of Alex.'

Very flushed, Sophie said: 'I shan't fall in love with your son, Madame.' She knew that with total certainty. All the passion she had to give had long ago been given to someone else.

'I hope not,' Madame said slightly drily. 'Or I shall have to dismiss you like your predecessors. You must always remember that you work for me, not Alex.'

'I'll remember,' Sophie promised firmly.

Madame pinched her cheek, looking pleased. 'Stand firm. I love my son, but he is a cannibal, gobbling other companies, devouring anyone who gets in his way. I couldn't live with Alex, Sophie. It would be like living in the same cage as a tiger—one would always be wondering when it would be one's own turn to be swallowed whole. You will discover in time that Alex wants to run my life for me. It will be your job to stop him. It won't be at all easy and you may feel in time that it would be much more pleasant for you to do as he wants, but you can't please both of us. You must make up your mind now that you are in my camp, not his.'

Sophie stared at her in astonishment. Madame met her gaze and smiled.

'You look dazed. Are you alarmed?'

'I hadn't expected the job to be so complicated,' Sophie confessed. 'What are the problems?'

'Problems? Only one,' said Madame. 'Alex. You will find out what I mean as time goes by—he will descend on us and demand of you that you tell him everything I have done since he last came. You will tell him nothing. Nothing at all, without my permission.'

Sophie bit her lower lip, frowning.

'He will demand an answer, he will rage, he will roar, he will turn lamb and smile at you, use his charm for all it is worth. You will tell him nothing, whether he uses threats or seduction.' Madame eyed her intently. 'Now, can you be firm, Sophie? Do you think you can handle my son?'

'I really don't know,' Sophie admitted wrily. 'I'll promise not to tell him anything without your permission, though. I think I can safely promise that.'

Madame patted her cheek, looking pleased. 'Good girl! I had the feeling you might do, that day we met. Although you have that hint of fire in your hair, your face is very disciplined for a girl of your age. By twenty-three, you know, most Greek girls are married with a family. Do you not want to marry?'

Sophie's face did not betray a thing. 'One day,' she said without expression.

'When you meet the right man?' said Madame, smiling.

Shrugging, Sophie smiled back. She had met the right man years ago, but things were not always that straightforward. Love could not be bestowed wisely or deliberately. When it came, one could only hide it if it came without hope, without a future.

The next twenty-four hours were hectic. Madame, as she had promised, took Sophie on a protracted shopping expedition, insisting despite her protests, on buying her a complete new wardrobe. 'You will be moving with wealthy people and you must look at home with them. I cannot have a secretary who looks as if she is badly paid.' Madame had a wicked smile when she chose and her eyes teased Sophie as she said that. 'Your own clothes are neat and pleasant, but they will not do now, Sophie.'

By the time they reached Crete Sophie felt completely disorientated, her brain whirling. It was dark as they drove up to the villa in the hills and all she could see through the car window was the rolling line of the hills against a plum-dark sky lit with steely stars which glittered far above them.

Welcoming hands guided Madame into the villa. Sophie stumbled after her, hearing the deep Greek voices all round her, aware of staring, curious eyes and barely conscious of the long, white building into which she followed her employer.

Only when she finally lay in her own room an hour later did she really take in the reality of being here. Greece, she thought, hearing the muted night sounds behind the lowered blinds. I'm really in Greece, and not just for a fortnight's holiday—for a year, at least. A whole wonderful magical year, she thought, smiling, and smiling still slid almost at once into deep exhausted sleep.

CHAPTER TWO

HER days at the villa soon fell into a tranquil, happy pattern. She got up early in the morning and swam in the pool which had been built on one of the terraced slopes of the large walled garden. At eight o'clock she had a continental breakfast in the sunny dining-room. Madame ate breakfast in bed and did not get up until nine. Sophie opened the post and glanced through the letters before taking them to Madame's sitting-room to take dictation of replies to those considered urgent. After that, Madame usually ordered her car and went out to visit people or keep some appointment. She was deeply involved in local charities and worked hard as well as contributing large sums of money to them. Sophie, left behind, typed the letters. If Madame did not return for lunch, Sophie ate alone with the two dark-garbed women moving behind her. They at first showed a certain offhanded indifference to her, but gradually they softened in their attitude. She was the first of Madame's secretaries who spoke Greek, she discovered, and she practised on Merina and Iris, their dark eyes laughing as she made elementary mistakes.

There were five servants. All of them had worked for Madame for years. They knew each other intimately, quarrelled noisily and adored Madame, who took a deep interest in all their families and was always ready to listen to their problems.

The gardener, Hector, was a gnarled old man with a wooden lined face tanned almost black by wind and weather, speaking little but spitting out his words at

Sophie's feet as though he despised her. 'So he does,' Madame told her, laughing, when Sophie mentioned it. 'Hector despises all women, even me.' Her thin shoulders shrugged. 'It is a Greek attitude which is passing, but the older men still regard women as beasts of burden, of no account. Hector has eight children and twenty-three grandchildren. His wife was a silent soul, God rest her. I used to have hard work getting a syllable out of her.'

Madame and Sophie often spent the afternoons sitting in the garden. During the winter they sat in a heated garden room, watching Hector slowly amass leaves, dragging his rough broom of bound twigs backwards and forwards on the lawns. When he had gathered them up he would heap them on to the compost heap hidden behind a low bush. Fallen branches would be burnt on a low bonfire, the thin blue smoke twisting up into the cold air.

Christmas came and Sophie felt a fleeting homesickness, the cards and parcels which arrived from her family making her eyes prick with tears. Alex Lefkas flew in to spend a holiday with his mother, surprising Sophie by giving her a present when he passed some gaily wrapped parcels to Madame.

Stammering, 'I'm afraid I didn't expect——' she was cut short in his peremptory fashion.

'Open it.'

Sophie unwrapped it and looked in delighted amazement at the large glossy book on Greek art. 'Thank you,' she said, glancing up at him.

He inclined his black head without comment and turned to watch his mother as she opened and exclaimed over the gifts he had brought her.

He only stayed two days and Sophie scarcely saw him during the time he spent there. She was careful to keep out of his way, remembering his mother's warning about him, leaving him alone with his mother as much as possible.

Just before he left he strode into the small office she used and glanced round in that narrowed stare before looking at her as she waited for him to explain his presence.

'Now, let me see my mother's accounts,' he said with a smile which Sophie could well imagine had wrought wonders with his mother's previous secretaries.

Sophie gave him a polite smile. 'They're in the safe, Mr Lefkas, and your mother has the key.'

'Get it,' he said, still smiling.

Sophie kept her own smile pinned to the face. 'Certainly.' She lifted her phone and rang Madame's sitting-room on the internal line. Madame answered and Sophie said coolly: 'Mr Lefkas wishes to see your accounts, Madame. Can I come and get the key to the safe?'

Alex Lefkas shifted his feet, his body poised menacingly, muttering something in harsh Greek under his breath. Sophie understood what he had said. She had heard Hector using language like that when he pruned a rose too closely and sheared off part of his thumb.

Madame laughed softly. 'Tell him to ask me for it,' she said. 'Is he with you?'

'Yes, Madame,' said Sophie, her face a smiling mask.

'Put him on,' Madame ordered.

Sophie offered him the telephone, her green eyes blank. 'Your mother wishes to speak to you, Mr Lefkas.'

He snatched the phone, giving her a look which should have gone right through her. Sophie listened to the rapid explosion of Greek which followed, her face carefully without expression. Alex Lefkas flung the phone down and turned to her, snarling.

'I obviously should have spoken to you myself before you came out here, Miss Bryant. I want you to listen now and understand me clearly. Whatever my mother has said to you, I am your employer. You will take my instructions, not hers. If there is anything I want to know, you will tell me. You will show me anything I want to see. You will do whatever I tell you to do. Is that clearly understood?' His grey eyes were fixed on her face, glittering fiercely.

Sophie looked at him calmly. 'I understood you, Mr Lefkas, but I hope you will try to understand me. I work for your mother, not for you, and I will do what she tells me to do. I'm sure I don't have to explain to you that I have no choice. My loyalty is to Madame, first and foremost. She made her wishes very clear to me when I first started work, and I shall follow them to the letter.'

He put both hands on her desk and bent towards her, his hard mouth tight. 'Listen, you obstinate female, I have to protect my mother against her own generous nature. God knows what she would get up to if I didn't keep my eye on her. She gives everything she has if it's asked of her. I won't let her bankrupt herself. If you won't co-operate with me, I shall have you dismissed.'

Sophie didn't flinch from the menace in the grey eyes or the distinctly dangerous look of the wide shoulders. 'That is obviously your prerogative, Mr Lefkas. I can only do what I think is right. If you think your mother's mind is unbalanced perhaps you should get the power of attorney which will give you the legal right to search all her papers.'

'What?' he roared, his black head lifting. 'I didn't say my mother's mind was anything but perfectly balanced. What the hell do you mean?'

'If Madame is sane, she surely has a right to do as she pleases with her own money,' Sophie said quietly.

'Who are you to tell me what rights my mother has or does not have? What if in a few months' time she has given away a fortune to someone with a sob story?'

'I'll try to see that she doesn't do that,' said Sophie, after a pause for thought. 'If I genuinely think she's giving away fortunes I shall get in touch with you.'

'You think I'm going to leave it like that?' He straightened and stared at her furiously. 'You really think I'm going to let you use your own judgment in a matter as important as this?'

Sophie didn't answer, looking at him calmly.

'You can pack your cases, Miss Bryant,' Alex Lefkas bit out through his firm white teeth. 'You'll be on the next flight back to England.'

Sophie lifted the phone. His long sinewy hand clamped down over hers and the grey eyes glared. 'What are you doing?'

'Ringing your mother to say goodbye,' Sophie said sweetly.

What he said then was again in Greek, and Sophie felt colour rise in her cheeks at the language.

He moved away, his back to her, the long graceful line of his body held stiffly as though rage were coursing through his limbs. She sat and waited, watching the black head.

It swung back towards her. His face was controlled again, the eyes cold but deadly.

'I'll remember this,' he said, then slammed out of the room. He left an hour later and Madame came into the office smiling, her eyes very bright.

'I hope my poor Alex is not going to suffer indigestion all the way to New York,' she said. 'He was in the nastiest temper I've seen him in for years.'

'I hope I didn't offend him too much,' Sophie said.

Madame met her green eyes and laughed down at her. 'I believe you don't care if you did or not!'

Sophie hesitated, then her eyes lit with laughter. 'Not much,' she agreed.

'I hope you keep that frame of mind,' said Madame. 'Because if I know Alex, he'll be back.'

It was, however, three months before they saw Alex Lefkas again. He came in the spring when the hills were a vivid startling green and wild flowers sprang everywhere in field and roadside. Crete was an island dominated by the mountains which rose in the centre of it, always capped with snow in the long winter, the massive glowering darkness of the rocky horizon never lightening in the dark days before spring.

Spring broke suddenly, the pastures hidden deep in the mountain valleys overflowing with flowers and new grass, the air clear and bright, scented with sweetness, the sky suddenly so blue it made one blink whenever one looked up at it. Even Hector almost smiled as he moved in his stolid way round the garden.

The glass top of the heated pool was rolled back and sunshine danced on the blue water as Sophie took her morning swim. She rose even earlier to enjoy the first cool hours of the day before the sun rose in the sky.

Floating idly on her back one morning, she heard a step on the tiled surround and looked round in surprise to see Alex Lefkas watching her. The next moment he had uncoiled like a spring in the air and somersaulted into the water, his long lean body cutting the blue surface and streaking away past her wordlessly. Sophie swam towards the side, retreating in faint alarm before his presence, but as she was about to haul herself out of the water his hand caught and seized her ankle, pulling her backwards. Splashing in confusion, she surfaced again, looking at him in amazement.

'Where were you going?' he asked, turning that smile on her, the flashing brightness of his eyes dazzling.

'To have breakfast,' she said, stammering slightly.

'Plenty of time,' Alex Lefkas retorted. He trod water, eyeing her speculatively in her demure swimwear. Madame had warned her that there would be lifted brows if she swam in the house pool wearing anything too revealing. 'We mustn't shock Hector,' she had said, laughing.

The yellow costume clung like a second skin to Sophie's body, outlining her firm breasts, small waist and slim hips. She was still pale after wintering here, her skin smooth and creamy where the swimsuit ended at her thighs.

'Charming,' Alex Lefkas murmured softly, lifting his grey eyes to smile into hers, the intimate glance catching her by surprise.

Warily, she eyed him. This, she thought, was phase two of his campaign to get his own way; his mother had warned her.

'How do you like living in Crete?' he asked.

'Very much.'

'You haven't been lonely, living here with my mother?' He kept his eyes on her, the thick black lashes giving his grey glance a fascinating excitement Sophie was not unaware of, despite her distrust of him.

'Not at all.'

'It's a very quiet life for a beautiful girl,' he said smoothly. 'Don't you miss London?'

'No.' Not an inch, she thought. She had barely even thought of the city since she left it. She felt too much at home in the villa with Madame and the quarrelling, laughing servants whose noisy life made such a contrast to the calmness in the part of the house where Madame and Sophie spent their days.

'While I'm here we must drive over to Heraklion and sample the best of Cretan cooking. There's a good hotel there which has a chef who really knows how to cook.'

Sophie's calm face did not alter by a flicker. 'Madame will enjoy that,' she said. 'She loves going out to dinner.'

She felt his grey eyes harden and narrow sharply. There was a brief pause, then he put a long finger on her bare arm and slid it smoothly down to her elbow, smiling at her, the grey eyes mocking. 'Not my mother, Miss Bryant, just you and I. We must get to know one another much better.'

Sophie moved very slightly so that his arm fell to his side again. 'How thoughtful,' she said. 'But you're here so rarely, Mr Lefkas. I wouldn't want to deprive your mother of your company even for a few hours.'

Turning, she climbed out of the pool and walked away to where she had left her robe. She heard him thrust with his legs, the water splashing as he got out of the pool. Sophie tied her belt tightly around her waist and turned to go, but Alex Lefkas stepped in front of her, the charm and smiling intimacy gone from his hard face.

'Let me give you a piece of advice, Miss Bryant. Don't make an enemy of me unless you can help it. I make a bad enemy but a very good friend.' His grey eyes bored down into her own. 'If you're wise you'll want me as a friend, I assure you.'

Sophie surveyed him warily. 'I've no wish to make an enemy of you, Mr Lefkas. All I ask is that you leave me alone to get on with my job. I'm very attached to your mother. You can rely on me to protect her as much as I can in every possible way.'

He didn't answer, but stared at her, his black brows level. Sophie walked away into the bright spring sunshine, hoping that was that. She did not want to embark on a long duel with Alex Lefkas, but she had given her word to his mother. One could not divide one's loyalties.

He had arrived overnight, she found, when she spoke

to his mother later. 'Typical!' Madame sighed. 'Just arrived at midnight. He was in Athens and took a
helicopter after having dinner with friends. I didn't even
know he was here until he strolled in on me while I was
still waking up! The way he dashes around the world
you'd think he would get dizzy!'

Madame stayed at home that day and Sophie carefully left mother and son alone all morning. At lunch Alex
Lefkas behaved perfectly, very courteous, smiling at her
whenever he caught her eye, pressing fruit upon her
when she refused the creamy dessert which the cook had
sent up.

When he suggested to his mother that he take her and
Sophie to Herklion to dinner, Madame smilingly shook
her head. 'I am dining with Ariadne. Why don't you
take Sophie?'

Alex Lefkas turned mocking eyes on Sophie. 'She
seems reluctant to risk spending any time with me,
Mama. What have you been telling her? Have you filled
her head with horror stories about me?'

Slightly flushed, Sophie angrily met his teasing
eyes. Madame laughed and said, 'Sophie is the best
secretary I've ever had, Alex. Don't turn her head, if
you please. I want her just the way she is—her brains
unscrambled. I know the effect you have on secretaries,
remember.' Her dark eyes glinted at him and he laughed
drily.

'Could I help it if a foolish girl took a few courtesies
so seriously?'

'You're a flirt,' said Madame, without real censure.
'But I won't have you flirting with Sophie.'

Alex Lefkas glanced sideways at Sophie, the grey
gleam of his eyes visible through his long black eye-
lashes. 'Is she susceptible?'

Madame viewed her complacently, smiling. 'Do you

know, I don't think she is, Alex. I think your much-advertised charm would fail on Sophie.'

Sophie finished her coffee, very irritated with the way they were discussing her in front of her, but keeping a calm expression on her face all the same.

'We'll see,' said Alex Lefkas, his voice amused.

Sophie's eyes briefly touched his face, a flash of angry green fire which made his eyes widen and brighten.

Madame came to her room that afternoon and insisted on choosing her dress for her. 'I want you to look your best when you dine with Alex. Remember, everyone will know you. Crete is a very small island and Alex is very well known.' Patting Sophie's cheek, she added softly, 'Don't weaken, child. When he turns that smile of his on you, remember, you work for me, not him. Alex will do everything he can to enslave you. It's how he operates. The two poor girls before you fell like nine-pins. I have high hopes of you, though. Like most Greek men, Alex firmly believes women are a second-class race. He would like to have total control of my whole life. He thinks because I am old I am foolish. He is wrong, but Alex would never admit to being wrong about anything. He has enormous pride and great self-respect—I wouldn't exactly call it vanity, but it is a strong belief in himself that can't admit to any weakness. Keep him at a distance.'

'Don't worry, Madame, I will,' Sophie said with absolute confidence.

Madame searched her green eyes curiously. 'You are so sure you are invulnerable. There must be a reason, Sophie. You never speak of anyone, but for you to have such confidence in your power to resist my son, you must either be a fool, which I don't believe, or you must care for someone else, so deeply that nothing Alex could do would ever undermine that feeling.'

Sophie felt herself paling, her eyes widening. Madame

was too clever, too shrewd. Looking away, Sophie said huskily, 'I shall not let your son talk me into being disloyal to you, Madame.'

Madame watched her for a moment, the dark eyes intent, then smiled at her, patting her shoulder. 'Very well, I shall ask no more questions. You have great dignity, Sophie. I know when a door is closed firmly in my face.'

Madame was dining with her oldest friend, Ariadne Stenessolos, who lived between the valley in which the villa lay and Knossos to the east. Hector's grandson drove Madame everywhere. When he and Madame had set off, Sophie went downstairs to find Alex Lefkas waiting for her impatiently, one eye on his watch.

He turned his black head in that abrupt gesture of his with which she was beginning to be very familiar and then the grey eyes fixed on her intently, taking in every detail of her appearance from the gleaming red-gold hair, past the simple but effective white gown in a Grecian style, to her silver strip sandals with their fine high heels.

Sophie was not easily put out of countenance, but she found the faint insolence of his inspection bringing colour to her cheeks. Her thin darkened brows lifted in silent comment on his deliberate appraisal and he looked back to her face to meet her irritated eyes with a dry little smile.

He was wearing an elegant white suit, the close fit of it emphasising the lean waist and long legs of a man in superb physical condition, his dark shirt fluted to give an impression of a jabot, a carefully tied white bow tie at his throat. The crisp black hair had been brushed until it lay smoothly back from his forehead.

'Ready?' he asked, making no comment on her appearance.

The drive down to Heraklion took them through the

wind-blown trees of a charcoal plantation, the holm-oaks hiding the pits in which the charcoal burners performed their task of rendering the wood down to the necessary residue with which cooking was usually done even now in Greece. Shadows flickered over Alex Lefkas's face as he drove. The dark roads wound narrowly, the surface rough and pitted. As they drove nearer to the sea the lights on the coast flickered like distant fires and the rush of the waves on the rocky shore, the smell of storm-draped weed around the rocks, began to make themselves felt.

Alex Lefkas glanced at her suddenly. 'You say very little, Miss Bryant. Is that because you have little to say or because you are wary of saying anything to me?'

'I barely know you, Mr Lefkas.'

'Alex,' he said softly.

She did not reply and he shot her another look. 'Is this another of my mother's rules? Are we to remain on formal terms for ever, Sophie?'

She considered that. 'Not necessarily,' she said, wondering how Madame would react if she began to use her son's Christian name.

'How gracious,' he mocked wryly.

She smiled faintly. 'I have no wish to be rude. I'm only following your mother's instructions.'

'Did she tell you why she has decided to make these stupid rules?' he demanded.

Sophie did not answer.

He laughed in a dry, amused way. 'I see she did. Can I be blamed if her last two secretaries imagined themselves to be in love with me?'

'As I wasn't here, I couldn't say,' Sophie returned. He knew very well that he was to be blamed, she thought. His manner to her had more than borne out his mother's accusation against him. He had been flirting with her ever since he arrived. The difference between his brusque, offhand manner on the day he interviewed her in London, his domineering arrogance last time he was here and the smiles and soft voice he was lavishing on her now was quite unmistakable—and totally phoney. Did he think she was a fool? You would have to be an idiot to be taken in by that deliberate, intimate charm which he turned on with such ease and complete cynicism.

They were treated with extreme respect at the large hotel in the centre of Heraklion. As the head waiter showed them, bowing, to a discreetly placed table behind a row of flowering shrubs in pots, Sophie was aware of eyes following Alex Lefkas avidly, the whispered comments running round the spacious dining-room.

They chose their food and sat talking over an aperitif until the first course arrived. Sophie was aware that Alex had altered his tactics slightly. His grey eyes still smiled whenever they caught her glance, but now he was quietly courteous, gently probing her thoughts with questions about her home and family, her friends, her life in London and her views of Crete. She answered calmly without saying very much, offering a blank wall to his occasional shooting stare.

He was trying to take her off her guard, she realised. He would lapse into silence, then suddenly ask her something personal without warning. Sophie never made the mistake of answering hurriedly; she would look down at her plate as though considering how to answer, then speak slowly and quietly.

He plied her with wine assiduously, refilling her glass whenever she drank some, so that she found it hard to keep track of how much she really was drinking. Realising that she was growing flushed and aware of a distinct slackening of her tense resistance to his questions, she avoided drinking any more, only pretending to sip at the glass. He watched her, eyes narrowed.

'You're very unusual, Sophie,' he said, leaning forward to smile at her, his hard face charming. 'Most girls of your age would be very bored living alone with an old woman in a quiet villa in the hills. Don't you ever yearn for the bright lights of London? Isn't there anyone in England you miss?'

'My family,' she said, watching the waiter pour their tiny cups of thick strong Greek coffee from the brass pot in which it had been brewed.

'Nobody else?' His black brows shot up, mockery in his eyes. 'No man, Sophie?'

She picked up a piece of sugar-dusted Turkish Delight and bit into it without answering him. The almond-flavoured straw-coloured sweet was so light it melted in the mouth.

'I'm sure your investigation gave you the answer to that,' she said a moment later, very coolly, giving him a faint smile.

His lips curled back to show those predatory white teeth. 'Would you object if I smoked?' he asked, and Sophie shrugged.

'Please,' she nodded.

He took his time lighting the cigar, the light blue wreath of smoke drifting away from him as he exhaled it. From behind the smoke he viewed her dispassionately. 'You're something of a mystery,' he said with a soft menace he did not bother to hide. 'I don't trust women who are as self-possessed as you, Miss Bryant. You've got to be hiding something. When I find out what it is, you'll be sorry if you have tried to pull the wool over my eyes.'

Sophie sipped her coffee before replying. Lifting her wide green eyes to his watchful face, she smiled at him, the curl of her mouth dismissing his threat. 'I assure you,

Mr Lefkas, I've no wish to pull the wool over your eyes.'

He leaned back with apparent casual relaxation, but his eyes were sharp and steely. After a moment he began to talk about the festivals she would be able to see in Crete that summer, the great saints' days which were marked by explosions of joy and delight all over Greece.

As they drove home across the island towards the villa, Sophie congratulated herself on getting through the evening without much trouble. She was, as she realised later, rather premature.

Following her into the villa, Alex said lightly: 'They will have left us a nightcap in the drawing-room.'

'No, thank you——' Sophie began, but he cut her short, taking her elbow and thrusting her through the door into the room. She looked at him with muted irritation. Who did he think he was? But she knew that. He was very much aware of who he was—and meant her to know it.

She sank on to the couch and watched him move to the decanters left on a delicately carved antique table. 'Brandy,' he said over his shoulder, making it a statement, not a question. Coming back towards her, he placed the full-bowled glass in her hand and stood in front of her, his black head tilted, tipping the smooth liquid down his throat.

Sophie sipped her brandy rather less rapidly, reluctant to drink it at all, aware that her head was slightly cloudy already. Alex began to talk about a concert he had heard in New York. 'Do you like Dvorak?'

'Yes,' she said, on the point of rising and going to bed.

'My mother tells me you enjoy browsing through our record cabinets. She's delighted to have a secretary who shares so many of her tastes.'

Sophie got up. 'Thank you. It was a very pleasant evening, Mr Lefkas, and I enjoyed the meal very much.'

She gave him a cool smile. 'Goodnight.'

She began to walk towards the door, but his hands fell on her shoulders and he whirled her towards him so fast that she had no time to protest before she was clamped against him in an intimate embrace. Lifting her head to look at him angrily, she met the mocking amusement in the grey eyes with irritation.

'Mr Lefkas——' she began, and his mouth closed over hers as she spoke, his lips moving exploringly. Sophie put her hands on the wide shoulders to disengage herself. 'Keep still,' he muttered, one hand now tilting her head, his fingers smoothing her flushed cheek.

Furious, Sophie brought her teeth together. He abruptly pulled his head back with a harsh exclamation.

'Why the hell did you do that?'

Sophie watched him probing the slight injury with one finger, his black brows drawn. 'My lip's bleeding,' he muttered, giving her a narrow-eyed glare.

'I'm sorry, but I'm not here for your amusement, Mr Lefkas. I'm here to work for your mother.'

She moved to the door, her slender body rustling in the soft folds of the white gown. The light glinted on her golden hair, bringing out all the fire hidden in the thick smooth strands.

Alex Lefkas stared after her, his eyes brooding. She went up to her room, smiling as she remembered his look of fury. Maybe now he would get the message and abandon his attempt to sway her allegiance from his mother to himself. She had some sympathy for his desire to protect his mother from herself—already Sophie knew that Madame was eager to help anyone who came to her with a tale of woe. Madame was generous, kind, open-handed. Sophie could understand Alex Lefkas's worry, but his mother was old enough to know what she was doing. She had her own income and if she wished to give it away,

Sophie felt that it was Madame's business.

Outside the laurels and cypresses whispered together as though they were laughing, and the wind rushed down from the mountains in great gusts, rattling the blinds at her window. Sophie forgot Alex Lefkas and went to sleep.

She half expected Alex to return to his offhand curtness with her next day, but when they met at lunch he gave her a flickering smile as he refused the lemon-flavoured soup he was offered. 'My lip is sore,' he said, and his mother looked at him in surprise.

'What happened?'

'Nothing of consequence,' he shrugged, taking a slice of smooth pâté.

Sophie bent over her soup. That described her perfectly as far as he was concerned, she thought drily. Nothing of consequence. And he meant her to know it.

He swam in the pool each morning, to her annoyance, and breakfasted with her, telling her stories of his boyhood in Crete, describing how the island had changed in the past twenty years. 'Not for the better,' he said. 'But it's the same everywhere. What civilisation gives with one hand it takes with the other. Now we have television the world is shrinking faster than we realise. The old clannish isolations are dying.'

'Much faster in a country like England,' said Sophie. 'Crete is still very much itself.'

'Custom dies hard here,' he agreed, and gave her a glinting, charming smile. 'You love it, don't you?'

'Very much,' she said, wary as she felt the deliberate nature of that charm. He watched her, still smiling, aware of her distrust.

Sophie was with Madame when Alex said goodbye to her. After kissing his mother and ordering her affectionately to look after herself, he gave Sophie a hard cool smile. 'Miss Bryant, keep an eye on her.' The words were ambiguous, the look in the grey eyes inimical.

'I will,' Sophie said drily, meeting his stare without flinching.

He nodded, staring at her expressionlessly now, then went with the rapidity he customarily showed when he moved into action.

Madame sighed, smiling. 'I love him, but he tires me,' she said. 'He is like a typhoon. One can only wait until it blows itself out or one is torn to shreds.' Her dark glance sharpened on Sophie. 'So, you did resist him,' she added, surprising Sophie.

Lifting her fine brows, Sophie asked: 'How do you know?'

Madame laughed. 'Alex was very irritated with you.'

'I'm sorry,' said Sophie, half smiling.

'I'm delighted,' Madame told her. 'You are a pearl beyond price, Sophie. At least now we can look forward to some peace again.' She looked at her curiously. 'I hope you will not find that boring.'

'I shan't,' Sophie assured her. 'I haven't been so happy for years.'

Madame sighed and Sophie looked at her in surprise. 'What's wrong?'

'You, Sophie,' Madame said. 'It isn't a natural way for a girl of twenty-three to think. You should be bored with the villa and our quiet days and nights. You should have lovers and the heady excitement of the world around you. I'm old, I am making my soul. But you are young, far too young for this life.'

'Perhaps I'm making my soul, too,' Sophie said lightly. 'Does one have to be old to do that?'

'Perhaps I shouldn't have warned you against Alex,' Madame murmured, glancing at her. 'Perhaps I should have let him play with your heart. Even a little heartbreak is better than no feelings at all.'

Sophie smiled wryly, her eyes rueful. 'It would have made no difference. I was never in any danger from your son, Madame.'

'No,' Madame said thoughtfully, eyeing her in that sober way. 'I wonder why.'

CHAPTER THREE

MADAME was quite wrong when she told Sophie that they would not see Alex again for months. Six weeks later he returned unexpectedly, but this time he brought guests with him and they had twenty-four hours' warning before he descended on them from the skies in a yellow helicopter. It whirled around the house like a noisy metallic dragonfly before it landed in the flat field beside the garden, startling the flock of sheep which grazed nearby and filling the valley with their nervous bleating as they skipped as far away as they could from the strange monster which had fallen from the skies.

The servants had prepared four rooms, as Alex had ordered, and they peered curiously from the back of the house as the visitors came through the front door.

Sophie was in her office. She heard Madame's voice greeting the guests, heard husky female laughter and deep Greek male voices. Alex Lefkas spoke above them, giving his mother some message from an old friend, then they all moved away and a door closed, silencing the sound of their talk.

Sophie went on with her work, forgetting them. She heard them later going to their own rooms to change and rest before dinner. The afternoon sun was sinking and cool blue shadows fell across the floor as she worked.

Glancing at her watch, she realised it was getting late and covered her typewriter. She was compiling a complete list of the charities in which Madame was interested with the comparative figures of her donations to them. When the door opened she looked up, a smile on her face, expecting to see Madame, but it was Alex.

Sophie's smile faded. She slid the papers she had just typed into their folder and quickly put them into a drawer and locked it.

'Don't hide things from me as if I were a spy come to steal the state secrets!' Alex snapped angrily, moving forward.

Sophie lifted her bright head, her eyes meeting his without a flicker. 'I was just tidying up before I went to change,' she said.

'And don't lie to me,' he bit out. 'What was that? What were you determined I shouldn't see?'

'You're imagining things,' Sophie said coolly.

'Show me, then,' he ordered, reaching out one peremptory hand for the key to the drawer which she was just sliding into her handbag.

Sophie smiled as though he were joking. 'Excuse me, Mr Lefkas,' she said, stepping round him.

He caught her arm, his fingers tight around her elbow, and the hard face stared down at her. 'Missed me?' he asked.

Sophie looked at him levelly, one brow moving upwards. Her silence brought a sudden dark flush to his face.

'I've worked you out, Miss Bryant,' he said. 'You're just a frigid little bitch with ice-water in her veins.'

'Thank you, how kind,' Sophie said drily, looking down at his detaining hand. 'Excuse me, Mr Lefkas, I have to change for dinner.'

He didn't release her, though. Watching her coldly he said: 'My mother sings your praises every time I speak to her, but don't imagine you will twist me round your little finger the way you do her.'

Sophie laughed. 'My imagination wouldn't stretch that far,' she told him.

'You don't fool me,' he said rapidly. 'No woman with your looks could be contented leading such a quiet life, unless she had some motive which made the boredom worthwhile.'

Sophie didn't bother to answer that, and after a pause, as though waiting for her to answer, he released her and moved to open the door, standing back to let her pass.

His guests were a married couple who worked for the Lefkas firm in Athens, Stephan and Helen Miklos, both of them in their thirties, and a brother and sister who also worked for the firm, but in New York. The Miklos couple were dark, quiet and friendly but not eager to say much. Patrice and Michel Lerrand were of French birth but had lived in the States for years, almost all traces of their origins lost in American accents. Michel was tall, with curly dark hair, his figure rather willowy and graceful. His sister was a good head shorter, a petite brunette, her flame-red dress startling in style and cut, revealing her breasts almost to the nipple. Sophie caught Madame's wry expression as she introduced the girl and was amused. Madame's tolerant sophistication found Patrice slightly jarring.

'Do you like working in Greece?' Patrice asked, eyeing Sophie's demure lemon dress with complacence.

'Very much.'

'Sophie is an excellent secretary, the best I ever had,' Madame said with a smile.

Alex moved to the decanters. 'What will you drink?' he asked Sophie over his shoulder, his eye flicking towards her, a glint of hostility in it.

'Sherry, thank you,' said Sophie, noting that that was what the other women were drinking.

He came back and put the glass into her hand, then turning his back on her almost insolently, he took Patrice's arm and said intimately: 'Come and tell me what you think of the Picasso sketch I've just bought.'

Sophie watched the charming smile he gave Patrice, her glowing-eyed response, and, glancing at Madame, was given a wink. Alex Lefkas had decided he was wasting his time on her, Sophie realised, and was turning his attention to more responsive quarry. It amused her that evening at dinner to have him ignore her, his profile turned towards her while he concentrated all his technique on Patrice, who hung on his every word, quivering with excitement, her eyes lustrous.

Under cover of discussing the meal, Michel Lerrand muttered to her: 'Quite a sight, Alex turning on the heat.'

'How old is your sister?' Sophie asked. Although Patrice had that sophisticated, daring gloss she looked rather young under her clever make-up.

'Twenty-one,' said Michel. 'I've warned her, but I'm afraid she isn't taking my warnings seriously.'

'Did you expect she would?' Sophie kept her voice down, murmuring the words into his ear, but at that moment Alex Lefkas turned his dark head and she felt the quick, cold shaft of the grey eyes. She turned her attention to her meal, flushing faintly at some expression in his face.

Madame went to bed as usual quite early, but Sophie sat with Michel Lerrand, laughing as he told her horror stories about New York in the rush hour, while Alex took Patrice out into the moonlit garden to admire the view of the mountains at night. Stephan and his wife quietly began dancing to a whispering tape of romantic music, smiling at each other. Catching her glance at them, Michel said smilingly: 'They've only been married a year and they're still in love.'

'How amazing,' Sophie mocked, laughing.

He grinned ruefully. 'That didn't come out right!' He

looked at the open french windows. 'I hope to God Patrice is keeping her cool. Alex is a flirt. I've known smarter girls than my sister make complete fools of themselves. They always think that this time it's different, that this time he's serious—and it's always the same.'

'You've obviously made a study of him!'

'I see quite a bit of him in New York. I suppose women find all that money irresistible—they can't help trying to grab him, but Alex is very elusive.'

'He's probably learnt to be,' Sophie said drily.

'I guess so,' Michel nodded in rueful agreement. He glanced at the other couple still circling sleepily. 'Shall we join them?'

'Why not?' she smiled, getting up.

They danced in silence, the room softly lit by a few lamps, the music low and sweet. After a few moments the Miklos couple smiled, said goodnight and drifted off to bed. Michel winked down at Sophie. 'As I said, they're still in love.'

'What exactly do you do in New York?' she asked him, and listened with interest as he described his job with Alex. Michel was clearly high up in the chain of command in the New York office, but he was unaffected, rather charmingly pleased with himself less for having risen so far than for being able to do the job itself.

'It isn't easy working for Alex,' he said with a grimace.

The curtains parted. Alex and Patrice came back into the room, Sophie felt Michel eye his sister grimly. She was flushed, eyes sparkling, her mouth somehow conveying the impression that she had been thoroughly kissed out in the darkness. Alex came behind her, his black brows jerking together as he glanced across the room. Sophie had her hands behind Michel's curly head as they circled, his hands on her slender waist. 'Do you have to work tomorrow?' Michel asked softly. 'Could you give me a guided tour of this part of Crete?'

The music suddenly stopped. Looking round, they saw Alex by the tape deck. His face expressionless, he said: 'I'm sorry, but the music might disturb my mother.'

Sophie unlatched herself from Michel, smiled a good-night at him and left the room. Alex Lefkas followed her into the hall, calling her back in an imperious voice.

She stopped, her face glancing back at him over her shoulder, the low lights sending a shadow over her skin. 'Yes, Mr Lefkas?'

He moved towards her, his hands in his pockets. 'I overheard Lerrand asking you to show him the hills. There is no question of you taking time off to amuse yourself with him. As you said to me yourself, you are here to work for my mother and not for any other reason.'

Sophie nodded coolly. 'Goodnight, Mr Lefkas,' she said, turning away.

He asked abruptly, 'Do you find him attractive?'

Sophie glanced back in surprise. 'Michel? Yes, he's quite attractive.'

She waited, but Alex Lefkas seemed to have nothing further to say. He turned away on a sharp movement and went back into the room where his guests were gathered. Sophie went up to her own room and got ready for bed. It was a long time before the others went to bed. She was asleep by then, but the whispered voices woke her briefly. She glanced at the clock and raised her brows as she saw that it was three in the morning. She hoped they had not woken Madame who had to get as much rest as possible.

Waking at her usual hour, Sophie slipped into her swimsuit and went down to the pool. She was astonished to find Alex Lefkas already there, swimming in a desul-tory fashion, lying on his back and moving his arms slowly as his body cruised from one end of the pool to the other.

He ignored her as she slid into the water and, imagining that he did not intend to speak to her, Sophie ignored him. She started to do her usual laps of the pool, swimming strongly, but after three turns Alex surfaced beside her before she could start off again and stared at her, pushing back the wet strands of thick black hair with a brusque movement of his hand. 'Did you sleep well?' he asked with what she could almost have said was a sneer, although why he should sneer at her on such a subject she couldn't imagine.

'Yes, thank you,' she replied, looking back at him. 'You're up early. I thought you would all sleep late this morning.'

His eyes flickered to her face, sharpening oddly. 'Did you hear us come to bed?'

'You woke me up,' she said, smiling slightly at him. 'But it didn't matter, I went back to sleep almost at once. I sleep very well.'

He gave her a look that astonished her, his eyes so fierce he looked as if he wanted to hit her, then turned and swam away without a word. Sophie stared after him, puzzled and half irritated, then shrugged her shoulders. He was the oddest man she had ever met, totally unpredictable and totally inexplicable. She continued with her steady laps of the pool. She was trying to build up the number she could do without getting tired. So far she had managed to do fifteen, but that had been on a morning when she felt particularly energetic. This morning she stopped at eight and paused, a hand on the side, breathing fast.

Heaving herself out of the water, she walked to get her robe. Alex Lefkas appeared beside her as she tied it around herself.

'Don't forget what I told you,' he said curtly. 'You are to work as normal while my guests are here. No wandering off with Lerrand when my back is turned.'

Sophie nodded indifferently, moving without answering him. He snatched up the black terry robe which he had left on a chair and came up behind her, shrugging into it, his broad shoulders gleaming wetly as he pulled the cloth over them.

'Lovely girl, Patrice, isn't she?' he asked her idly.

'Very beautiful,' Sophie agreed. Was he perhaps more taken with Patrice than Michel feared? He had spent some time out in the moonlight with her last night, obviously kissing her senseless from the look of her as she came back into the house again.

Keeping pace with her as she walked rapidly towards the villa, Alex asked her: 'Have you ever seen a sexier figure?'

'Not lately,' said Sophie, half laughing. Or so much of it on show, she thought, her green eyes lowered to hide the amusement in them. But if that was what turned him on ...

'Fantastic legs,' commented Alex, sliding a look at her sideways.

'I'm not a connoisseur of legs,' Sophie said gravely.

She heard his teeth snap together suddenly and looked round in surprise. The grey eyes were flinty. 'You seem to find something funny,' he accused. 'Perhaps you'd like to share the joke.'

Sophie regarded him with bewilderment. 'There's no joke,' she said calmly.

Why on earth was he looking at her like that? She could feel waves of black rage coming out of him. He was simmering like a volcano about to erupt, his eyes glittering at her, his mouth twisted, his features held under a vice-like pressure which indicated tremendous wrath about to blow sky-high.

For a moment she was alarmed by the look in his eyes, then he turned and walked into the villa like someone marching into battle. Sophie followed more slowly, thinking that she would not be sorry when Alex Lefkas and his guests packed up and departed.

Michel popped his head round her office door halfway through the afternoon. The house party had spent the day with Alex driving in the hills, but they had arrived back a short while ago, their loud voices disturbing the usual calm peace of the villa.

Madame was resting on her bed. 'Alex is worse than ever,' she told Sophie. 'Really, every time he comes here he gets more intolerable! I've had the most appalling quarrel with him over you this morning. He wants me to sack you.'

Sophie hadn't been surprised. 'Are you going to?' she asked, smiling.

Madame laughed at her. 'No. When I told him I refused, he almost blew up.'

'What does he accuse me of?' Sophie asked curiously.

'Everything from dumb insolence to flirting with Michel Lerrand,' Madame said slyly, glancing at her. 'He seems to feel that that is your worst offence. He said you don't know your place, you give yourself airs, you're arrogant, high-handed and opinionated. He also said if he catches you with Michel again he didn't care what I said, he would fire you.'

'I'll keep out of Michel's way,' Sophie promised, shrugging.

'Nonsense,' Madame said in that soft amused voice, grinning at her. 'Flirt with Michel as much as you like, Sophie. Take no notice of Alex. Why shouldn't you have a little fun? While our guests are here there's no need for you to do anything at all. Enjoy yourself.'

Sophie had not taken the command seriously. Now, looking back at Michel with a smile, she said: 'Have a good time?'

'Very enjoyable,' Michel said, coming further into the room. He perched on the edge of her desk. 'Can't you stop work for the day?'

'I'm here to work,' Sophie said lightly.

'All work and no play,' Michel suggested, his dark eyes on her glittering red-gold hair. 'I've never seen such hair. It is an amazing colour.' Leaning over, he picked up a soft strand and let it run through his fingers, watching the sun catch it and sparkle.

The door was flung open behind them. Michel looked round and his face showed surprise and alarm as he caught Alex's harsh stare. Sliding off Sophie's desk, he mumbled something and moved to the door. Alex said through his teeth: 'Miss Bryant is here to work, Michel, not to flirt with you.'

Michel scurried out, his willowy body vanishing at top speed. Alex slammed the door after him and then turned on Sophie, the black brows heavily menacing above the cold eyes.

'I thought I told you to stay away from him?'

'I haven't moved away from my desk,' Sophie pointed out.

'He was in here.'

'I could hardly ask one of your guests to leave.'

'Do so next time,' Alex said bitingly.

Sophie regarded him in dry disbelief. 'You really expect me to dismiss one of your guests from my office?'

His expression changed. He sauntered across the room and sat on the side of her desk close to her, his thigh touching her knee. Sophie shifted in her chair so that their bodies no longer touched and Alex gave her a hard, derisive grin. 'You seem to have no trouble dismissing me,' he said mockingly.

Sophie looked away from those teasing eyes. 'Please, Mr Lefkas, I thought we'd been through all this,' she said with impatience in her voice.

'All what?' he demanded.

'You know very well what I mean.'

'I don't. Tell me.' The grey eyes were wandering over her as he spoke in leisurely and apparently pleasurable inspection. He was smiling as he took that lengthy tour of her face and body and Sophie tensed with irritation at the sexual appraisal he made no attempt to hide.

'I'm working,' Sophie muttered, flushing under the deliberate, sensual stare.

'I'm not surprised Lerrand was fascinated by your hair,' he told her, leaning forward and capturing a handful of it.

'Don't!' snapped Sophie, reacting angrily, pushing his hand away.

It was like dropping a match on to petrol. Alex drew a thick, angry breath, staring down into her face, then he pulled her up out of the chair, his hands behind her shoulder-blades, holding her in a proximity which she could not escape, his eyes a few inches from her own as he fixed her furiously with intent accusation.

'It won't work,' he bit out, and Sophie stared up at him in total incomprehension.

'What are you talking about?' She was tense and stiff in the circle of his arms, wondering what it would take to make this maddening man leave her alone.

'Do you think it hasn't been tried before? And by lovelier women than you, Miss Bryant.' His mouth curled in a taunting smile. 'I'm far too experienced to be taken in by the old flight and pursuit game, so why waste time on it? If you're holding out to whip up my interest, don't bother.'

Sophie's skin ran with angry colour and her eyes flashed a bright hard green. 'Mr Lefkas, you're under a misapprehension. I'm not trying to intrigue or attract you. I have no interest in you whatever. All I want is to be left to do my job in peace.' She pushed at his shoulders, wriggling to escape. 'Now, will you let me go?'

'Will I hell!' he muttered savagely, a dark red invading his face. She tried to evade the searching mouth and he wound his hand in her thick golden hair, pulling her head back so that she gasped in protest, then his lips forced themselves down against her own. For the first moment she was merely rigid with anger and she could feel the anger in Alex Lefkas as he kissed her. His lips meant to hurt. They ground her lips back against her teeth until the inner lip split and blood seeped into her mouth. Sophie had never been kissed like that before. She was very conscious of the punishment which the kiss was intended to inflict. Her own blood salted her tongue, she quivered with insult and rage.

Abruptly it changed. Alex moved closer so that she felt the hard pressure of his long body against her. His hand curved round her nape and stroked it sensually. His mouth softened, coaxed, shaping her lips under his own passionately while his other hand slid down her body in a caressing exploration which brought her stinging to life.

Wrenching herself away she faced him, trembling angrily. 'How dare you manhandle me? Keep your hands to yourself! You brought Patrice Lerrand here for your amusement, presumably—stick to her. She seems to want your attentions, I don't!'

She saw the violent leaping eyes for a few seconds before his lids veiled them. His face tautened, all the excitement she had seen in it a moment before pushed out of sight, then he swung towards the door and left without a word.

Sophie could not work for some time. Alex Lefkas had disturbed and upset her too much for her to be able to concentrate on anything. She sat at her desk, shaking, her face hot, clenching and unclenching her hands.

Although she felt no desire for him whatever, the warm movements of his mouth on her own and the stroking hand which had run down her body had aroused other thoughts, other feelings in her.

She leaned her face in her hand, her eyes closed. It was very hard to force down the needs of her body, the aching longing of her heart. Love which has no expression, no outlet, can be forced into tormented shapes, grow strangely within the mind. Long ago she had told herself that she would forget the man whose image troubled her sleep, but she had found it impossible and given up the attempt. She had never felt desire for anyone else, but just now for one second as Alex Lefkas's mouth coaxed against hers she had felt a flicker of aroused excitement inside herself. The sensuality of which her body was capable had come struggling to the surface in that instant and now she felt it throbbing away inside her.

That evening she pleaded a headache to Madame and went to bed instead of going down to dinner, but she did not sleep; she lay awake, her mind tortured by thoughts of the man she loved, all the intolerable loneliness of the past five years tearing at her.

Madame had once said to her that she had a disciplined face. Sophie's mouth writhed miserably as she remembered that. Disciplined, she thought—oh, yes, that was true. She had learnt that discipline over years of pain, separation, refusal to weaken. The marks of that long struggle had worn away her flesh, imposed the

mask of strength on her face, given her the cool assur-
ance which hid from everyone she met the depth of pain
inside her.

It would have been so easy, so exquisitely satisfactory,
to begin a passionate affair with him which would have
gratified the needs they both felt. Nobody need ever have
known. How many nights had she lain awake telling herself she was a fool to deny herself the only thing she
needed, the only man who could ever make her happy?

In the beginning it had been almost too much to bear.
She had fought against the urge to give in to her burning
desire for him and hard as the struggle had been, she had
won. Gradually she had managed to slacken the taut
rope of her passion until in the past year or two she had
sometimes managed to keep his image from her mind for
days at a time.

It had not occurred to her until now that it was possible to feel aroused in any other man's arms. She had not
wanted Alex Lefkas, but he had forced her to feel a piercing thrust of sexual excitement, all the same. Her
emotions were too centred on another man for that excitement to be turned towards Alex Lefkas, yet her face
burned with heated shame as she remembered the feelings she had felt for that second.

It was a warm night, a night of spring but borrowed
from summer, the air moving languidly around the villa,
the moonlight clear and cool on house and garden. She
had opened her windows. The cicadas kept up their tire-
less music in the shrubs and trees. Staring at the sky, she
watched the soft grape-bloom colour deepen and shift as
the night wore on and the air cooled slightly.

Voices drifted up to her open window. She lay listening, recognising the deep notes of Alex Lefkas's voice
and the high light voice of Patrice. She waited for them
to move away, but the murmuring went on very close to

her window and she could not avoid hearing, understanding. Alex Lefkas was teasing Patrice and she was laughing excitedly.

Sophie heard the kisses he was giving the girl, knew from the way Patrice sighed and murmured that he was getting all the encouragement he had not got from her.

Irritated, Sophie got out of bed and silently went to the window to close it and drop the blind.

Her eye involuntarily slid down to the wide stone terrace beneath her window. She saw the black head bent, the gleam of white arms around his neck. Carefully she closed the window and let the blind close over the night. She heard only one thing more—Alex Lefkas laughing, softly, huskily, as though Patrice had delighted him.

Silence succeeded that. The night sounds wound their tranquil pattern into her ear and sleep came at last.

She had just completed her fifth lap of the pool next morning when she heard the splash with which Alex Lefkas entered the blue water. She looked round over her shoulder and saw his long, lean body uncoiling and flashing away through the pool.

A prickle of annoyance ran through her. The quiet mornings she was so used to in the pool were disturbed by his presence. He had certainly gone to bed very late. Didn't he need sleep like other people? Why didn't he take his guests and leave? He was destroying the safe harbour his mother had offered her here over the past months.

His black head shot past her, then he turned to throw her an aggressive little smile. 'Sorry if we disturbed you last night.'

Meeting those grey eyes Sophie suddenly knew it had been deliberate. He had stood under her open window and made love to Patrice with the intention of annoying her. She gazed at him blankly, her green eyes faintly curious. He really was an odd man! He was like a child who can bear anything but being ignored. She presumed his resounding success with other women in the past made her indifference galling.

'You didn't disturb me,' she said calmly after a pause.

As if her answer stung him he hardened his mouth. Raking his long hand through his wet black hair, he flattened it against his scalp, eyeing her with dislike.

'Let's be frank, Miss Bryant,' he said with open hostility. 'I don't trust you. You're too damned cool.'

Flaring at his tone, Sophie snapped back: 'If you mean I object to you mauling me around, it may be news to you, Mr Lefkas, but not all women like being man-handled!'

'Are you a feminist?' he demanded.

'Don't try to stick labels on me, I'm not a jam jar!'

He half laughed then glared at her. 'You're up to something, and I'll find out what it is one day. If you have ambitions of milking my mother, forget them. Every cent you get out of her you'll pay back with interest.'

Sophie's green eyes held distaste as she stared back at him. 'My God, can't you think of anything but money?' She turned to the side of the pool and clambered out, dripping on the tiles as she padded to get her robe. The sunlight danced and glittered on the water as Alex Lefkas lifted himself out of it to join her.

Sophie glanced up as she was wrapping her robe around her wet body and felt a dart of shock as she found his eyes fixed on her, narrowed and glinting. They lifted to meet hers and Alex Lefkas said softly: 'A clever girl like you could do very well for herself if she used her head. You're wasting your time here. Come to New York. I'll find you an apartment ...'

Hot colour rushed into Sophie's face as she realised what sort of offer he was making her. She broke into what he was saying, her voice unsteady. 'Don't say any more—the answer is no.'

He caught at her shoulder, his long fingers fondling the rounded curve of it as he looked at her with a practised, charming smile.

'There are always openings in the organisation for a clever woman with your sort of looks.'

'Oh, I can imagine,' Sophie muttered, pushing his hand away. 'But I'm not interested.'

'You're not indifferent to me,' he murmured in a voice which was slightly husky. 'Don't pretend you are.' The grey eyes were fixed on her mouth and he was breathing quickly. 'You're lovely. Even that cool little face of yours manages to suggest hidden fires, especially when those green eyes flash. Any man with blood in his veins is going to want to find out just how hot those fires are.'

Flushing to her hairline, Sophie said contemptuously, 'It would serve you right if I went straight to your mother and repeated this conversation.'

He straightened, his mouth hardening, the grey eyes boring into her. 'Are you blackmailing me?'

'Just try to get it through your thick head that I'm not interested in your proposition,' Sophie snapped. 'Keep your hands and your eyes to yourself!'

She turned away and walked out into the sunshine, leaving Alex Lefkas staring after her, his hands on his slim hips, a little pool of water forming around his bare feet.

She heard the whirring of the helicopter that afternoon and looked out of the window in surprise. Michel Lerrand popped his head round the door, resignation in his face. 'Well, we're off now.'

'Going so soon?' Sophie was astonished, then she began to laugh. 'With one bound Jack was free!'

Michel stared in confusion. 'What?'

'Never mind,' said Sophie. 'A little English joke.'

'Oh, one of those,' Michel said, laughing. 'I never get them.'

'They're not very funny,' she agreed.

'It was nice meeting you, even if for such a short time,' he said, and she smiled back at him.

'Maybe we'll meet again,' he went on, and Sophie nodded.

Alex Lefkas did not make an appearance. She saw his tall figure moving towards the helicopter ten minutes later, the black hair blowing wildly in the wind from the revolving blades. He bent and ran towards it with the others close behind him. A few moments later the machine lifted and Alex Lefkas was carried out of her life once more.

His mother considered her thoughtfully over dinner. 'That was a short visit,' she said.

'Your son is very unpredictable.'

Madame looked oddly amused. 'And sometimes very predictable,' she murmured, her eyes sliding to Sophie.

Did Madame suspect the sort of approach he had made to her while he was here? Sophie knew that, despite her sweetness and kindness, Madame was no innocent in the ways of the world, particularly the dog-eat-dog world in which Alex Lefkas lived and thrived.

They had talked about it sometimes. 'I prefer to stay out of that goldfish bowl,' Madame had told her. 'It's an artificial world where big fish prey on little fish and everyone wants to grab something from everyone else. These people cannot even breathe real air any more—they have air-conditioned homes because their lungs no longer work properly. They never walk, they ride in their cars everywhere, so their legs no longer function as they should. Look at their beautiful, gleaming faces and ask yourself: are they human? Each night they peel them off, and in the morning put on a new one. They are not faces, Sophie—they are beautiful, unreal masks which hide something ugly and selfish and small-minded. Their teeth are so white they dazzle you, but it is not a natural whiteness. Their high-paid dentists keep them like that, capping their rotting teeth with porcelain. Their bodies are sleek and smooth and they indulge them without compunction. But under all this, Sophie, are minds and hearts which are so empty they terrify you. The only emotions they know are greed and lust. The only thoughts they have are ones of self. Tiny stunted minds and tiny shrivelled hearts are all you'll find in those beautiful bodies.'

Sophie had listened soberly, watching Madame's thin lined face with compassion and admiration.

'Look around this island,' Madame had gone on, smiling at her. 'Look at the faces of the poor as they walk in the sun or ride on their donkeys up and down the steep hillsides. That is life. It leaves the marks of experience and pain, and it is real.'

Sophie had not felt even for a second any temptation to accept the future Alex Lefkas had offered her. She did not want to become one of the beautiful, pampered unreal women with which his world was peopled. He had nothing she wanted.

CHAPTER FOUR

Now that the warmer weather had come, Madame took Sophie on drives around the island several times a week. They went far afield, penetrating the secret green valleys which threaded through the mountains, their sides forested with pines haunted by cicadas, their windy fastness rarely visited by any but peasants on donkeys on their way to town.

Knossos was their target on some of the drives. Sophie always felt she had missed the core of it, however many times she went, walking through the ruins and marvelling at the technical skills Crete had possessed so many centuries before the rest of the world.

On hot summer afternoons they paused in one of the villages to sit at a taverna in the main square and drink a glass of clean cold water with their coffee. Often old women sat there, spinning, waiting for a passing tourist to stop and buy one of the shawls they made. The fine spider-web threads were soft in the hands, quickly shedding tufts of wool. Sophie told Madame the great clouds of white sheepswool with which the women worked looked to her like candyfloss at a fair.

'Ah, but those faces,' said Madame, smiling. 'Such strong dark faces; like the faces of saints in icons.'

There was always a church in the centre of each village. In the dark shadows glittered the icons, often decorated with silver leaf or gold, the Byzantine features melancholy, remote.

In front of one, Sophie exclaimed: 'He looks like Alex.'

Madame eyed the icon and smiled slightly. 'Yes, he does.' She sighed. 'Alex as he can be,' she added with open regret. 'As he is with me but with nobody else.'

The hard fierce face held pride, tenderness and strength, Sophie thought, staring at it. A very Greek face, memorable and haunting.

They had seen nothing of Alex since his sudden departure. He wrote to his mother, he sometimes rang her from New York. Sophie now and then answered the phone to hear his deep voice on the other end of the line. Although she realised that he knew very well who was speaking, he always pretended not to know, merely asking tersely for his mother.

One very hot afternoon Madame complained of a headache and went up to bed but came down again, a hand at her head, frowning. 'I feel restless,' she said, looking at Sophie with disturbed eyes. 'I can't think why. The air's so oppressive.'

'It's very hot,' Sophie agreed, watching the heat haze dancing on the horizon beyond the window.

'Humid,' said Madame. 'I hope we aren't . . .'

She never finished that sentence. Halfway through it Sophie felt the air vibrate with a sound she could not hear. The ground under her feet heaved, the trees swayed on the skyline.

'Sophie,' Madame said urgently, 'outside—earthquake!'

Sounds burst all round them—servants shrieking, tiles tumbling from the roof with ear-splitting crashes, glass shattering somewhere in the garden. But it was already all over. The air had settled again, the ground was stable. Madame, white and shaking, was put to bed again and Sophie soothed the excited servants as they argued and shouted at each other about what they should have done and had been too surprised to do.

Hector, grumbling vociferously, moved around sweeping up glass and tiles. Sophie walked down the lawns and looked around, to see nothing out of the ordinary and yet to feel a knowledge of the fragility of life. The quake had been a light, passing thing, but it could so easily have been very different. The smooth manicured lawns of the carefully tended garden could have been split wide open with the force of the earth beneath. 'The bull beneath the earth,' as Hector told her, 'tossing his horns and grumbling.' When he drank a glass of rough local wine later he spilled a few drops on the earth sideways, muttering in Greek—a libation of propitiation to the god beneath his feet, Sophie recognised, and could understand his need to do it.

It had all been over too quickly for her to panic, but the panic she had not felt then was welling up in her now, a sensation of the insubstantiality of life, the impermanence of it compared to the life of the ancient dark mountains around her.

Living here, with the unbroken traditions still kept by the Cretans, one was more aware of life than one was in a modern city where so much was artificial and man-made.

Madame did not get up again that day. Sophie ate dinner alone, a rather sparse meal of hummus followed by a stew made with octopus. She sat listening to music afterwards, the volume down so that she should not disturb Madame. The phone rang and Sophie hurried to pick it up, expecting one of Madame's friends to call, as they had been doing all day since the earthquake, to check that she was safe and well and to divulge in excited gossip what had happened in their part of Crete.

'Sophie?'

Recognising Alex's hard urgent voice she said quickly: 'She's quite all right.'

'I just heard on the telex from Athens,' he told her. 'What exactly happened?'

'It was nothing much. A little quake.'

'Is she there? Put her on.'

'She's asleep in bed,' Sophie told him, smiling. 'I've kept her in bed since it happened.'

There was a little silence. 'Thank you,' he said. Another pause. 'Were you frightened?'

'Not at the time. Later, a little, when I realised how it could have been.'

'Yes.' His voice was deep. 'You weren't hurt?'

'None of us was hurt. We had a few tiles dislodged and the cucumber frame was broken. Hector is very cross about it.'

'I can imagine,' he said, a smile in his voice. There was another little pause and he asked casually, 'I didn't wake you? You aren't in bed?'

'No, I was still up.'

'What are you doing?'

She looked at the receiver in surprise, having half expected him to ring off now that his worry about Madame had been dispelled. 'Listening to music,' she said.

'What are you listening to?'

'Can't you hear it? Yannis Markopoulos—the new LP. Your mother got it the other day.'

'You like Greek music?'

'I love everything Greek,' Sophie said, smiling.

'You've forgotten something, haven't you?' Alex murmured in a low, husky voice.

'What?' she asked in surprise.

'I'm Greek.'

She felt her skin run with hot colour, her breath drawn in a gasp of astonishment, and was very glad he wasn't in the room. It would have delighted him to make her blush.

She heard him laugh softly, as if he knew, as if he had heard the intake of her breath.

'Goodnight, Sophie,' he whispered.

The phone clicked. She sat there, staring at the receiver in her hand, her eyes confused. Maddening man, she thought, replacing it and putting her hands to her flushed face. He even flirts on the phone. He can't resist it, I suppose. He has to exert that fatal charm on every woman he meets. When he lowered his voice to that intimate, husky note however she tried to pretend she didn't notice, Sophie knew she did.

He rang again next morning. 'Sleep well, Sophie?' he asked with casual amusement, as though he knew he had disturbed her last night.

'Here's Madame,' she said, pretending not to have heard the question, quickly passing the phone to his mother.

Madame spoke to him cheerfully, assuring him she was perfectly well. 'It's still very hot here,' she said. 'But I expect we won't have any more trouble.' She paused, listening to whatever he was saying, then said: 'Nonsense, Alex!' Again she listened, her brow furrowed, then gave Sophie a quick sharp look before saying: 'Well, I'll think about it. Yes, Alex, I'll think about it, I promise you. Tomorrow? Yes, talk to me tomorrow.'

When she had rung off she looked at Sophie and asked: 'Do you miss London, Sophie?'

Smiling, Sophie shook her head, the light catching the tint of fire in the gold hair.

'Alex is worried about a second quake. Often another follows on and can be stronger, more dangerous. He wants to persuade me to leave Crete for a week or two, until the weather changes.' She eyed Sophie with quizzical amusement. 'Do you think you could bear a few days in London? You could visit your family while we are over there.'

Sophie's face tightened. 'It's your decision, Madame.'

Madame studied her. 'Well, we'll see, shall we? You have been happy here, haven't you, Sophie?'

'You know I have. I love Crete.'

Madame nodded. 'But I think perhaps we could both do with a change of scene. I can do some shopping in London and we could see a play or go to a concert. A break would be good for both of us.'

Sophie was not very keen on the idea, but if Madame wished to leave the island, she would obviously go with her, if Madame wanted her to come. Over the months while they shared the villa, she had become deeply attached to Madame Lefkas. The thin erect figure moving around the house and garden was always so endearing. Madame had a sense of humour, great kindness and a quick and clever mind. Sophie was never bored in her company.

Two days later they were flown to Athens in a helicopter sent by Alex to pick them up. They were on a flight to London that afternoon and Madame slept all the way. Reaching Heathrow, they made their way through Customs quickly and found a car waiting for them. Within eight hours of leaving the villa, they were at the penthouse suite kept for the use of the Lefkas family when they were in London. Sophie saw Madame to bed and talked to Vinny, the middle-aged woman who was in permanent charge of the suite. Vinny made her a light supper and then said goodnight before leaving for her own private part of the suite.

Sophie stretched out on the couch, exhausted by the flight yet too strung-up after so much activity and stress to be able to sleep. She had showered earlier and was ready for bed, but her mind just would not wind down.

Her golden head cushioned, she listened to low music, one arm curved above her, her bare feet wriggling thoughtfully as she tried to decide whether or not to visit her family while she was in England. Madame was insisting on it. Sophie had not let her see how reluctant she was to go for fear of arousing Madame's curiosity, but she was very conscious of the danger inherent in going home.

She would see him, hear his voice. It would be the same mixture of heaven and hell she knew only too well. Should she risk the upheaval which would follow? Months away from him and she almost forgot him. See him just once and she would fall back helplessly into the old vortex of anguish and desire.

A sound made her turn, lifting her bright head in a sleepy movement. Alex stood in the door, staring at her, his lean body outlined in light from the corridor outside.

Sophie stared in astonishment. Madame hadn't suggested that Alex might be here. Did she know?

He came into the room and closed the door, strolling towards her. Sophie began to get up, but he bent, a hand on her shoulder, pushing her back. 'No, don't move, you look far too comfortable.'

His eyes flickered over her, taking in the cream silk nightdress which her movement had revealed, the matching negligee she wore over it floating loose as she began to rise. Putting a hand quickly to the open folds, she pulled them across her body.

'Does Madame know you're here?' A faint suspicion darkened her eyes. Madame wouldn't have kept it from her. Would she?

Alex sat down, his thigh against her own, increasing her anxiety. 'I mentioned that I might be able to get over.'

Sophie frowned. Why hadn't Madame told her?

'Did you have a good trip from Athens?' Alex asked casually. He was wearing a dark business suit in a light material, his shirt open at the neck, the brown throat gleaming in the soft light.

'Yes, thank you. Madame went straight to bed.' Sophie's voice was stiff. She was wondering how without seeming panic-stricken she could extricate herself from this far too intimate situation. She did not like the quick, flicking movement of his eyes as they shot from her face to the tense length of her slender body on the cushions of the couch.

'Weren't you tired?' His long, sinewy hand reached out as he spoke and began playing with the bow of her negligee, flicking the ribbon with one nail.

'Yes, I am, actually,' she said hurriedly, sitting up, but that brought her far too close to him because Alex refused to budge, his face inches from her own, a faint smile on the hard mouth.

Somehow the bow had come undone. She looked down, startled, as the negligee fell back. Alex's grey eyes were on the half-revealed golden skin of her shoulders and breasts, warmed and coloured by the Cretan sun for the last few months. Before she could stop him his hand curled round one of her breasts, tugging down the soft silk and baring her nipple.

'Get your hands off me, damn you!' Sophie burst out, furious, her face scarlet.

His long finger stroked dexterously, and she gave a stifled gasp, shaken by the pleasure the movement sent through her. The hardening of her nipple under his caress told him too much. With a quick, harsh sound he bent his black head and Sophie fell back, trembling, as she felt the warm moistness of his mouth taking possession.

'No, please,' she almost whimpered, but although she

made the protest her eyes had closed and she was quivering as his head moved against her.

The intensity of her own reaction took her entirely by
surprise. Quick, piercing stabs of sexual excitement were
shooting through her body. Years of disciplined supres-
sion dissolved in a few seconds. She lay on the couch
moaning, twisting restlessly, barely sensible of Alex
lowering himself beside her, his hands moving quickly,
exploringly.

His head moved up and he opened her mouth, feeding
urgently on her surrendered lips. She felt the hard pressure as he rolled on to her, his thigh on hers, his hands
trembling as they fondled her breasts.

He had turned up at precisely the wrong moment. She
had been lying here tortured by need and passion for another man, her senses flaming, and Alex Lefkas was
reaping that harvest.

She wasn't even able to think; she was too aroused.
She had wound her arms round his neck and was kissing
him back with a heat and urgency which grew with his,
their bodies clamped together, the drive for satisfaction
deepening with every movement.

Breathing thickly, Alex sat up and flung off his jacket,
beginning to take off his shirt, his hands trembling as he
tore the buttons loose. Sophie forced her eyes open,
shuddering in the aftermath of a sexual onslaught which
left her chilled and shocked. Realising with a rush of
guilt and shame what would happen if she didn't do
something to stop him, she leapt up. Alex swung, face
darkly flushed, stopped her as she tried to get past him,
his hand catching her waist.

'Where are you going?'

'I can't,' Sophie whispered thinly.

'You can't stop now! My God, are you trying to drive
me crazy?' The grey eyes were flintlike, hard and glit-

tering, his features taut with a desire which made his voice sound hoarse.

'I'm sorry,' she groaned, staring at him.

'Sorry?' He said that through his gritted teeth, a savagery coming into his eyes. 'You're sorry? You're doing it deliberately! It's a well-orchestrated little campaign, isn't it? Do you think I don't know how it goes? You tease me, intrigue me, keep me running after you without ever letting me get too close, then when I'm going out of my mind, you almost let me catch you so that I'm at fever pitch and ready to give you anything.' His eyes narrowed to points of fierce steel. 'Well, I refuse to let you play games with me, you provocative little bitch. You're not leading me on and then ditching me just when I think I'm getting somewhere at last. You've come this far, you can go the whole way!'

'Get your hands off me!' Sophie flared, frightened and angry, her eyes dilating.

'My hands are going where I choose, not where you dictate,' Alex muttered with that thick intonation increasing as his eyes kept moving over her. 'My God, I want you. Your body has been driving me mad for months.' His hand slipped intimately down the curve from breast to thigh. She heard his breathing quicken, saw with dismay the burning intensity of his stare. Shrugging out of his shirt, he threw it down to the carpet. 'Face it, Sophie,' he whispered as he bent towards her. 'You've lost your gamble. I claim the stakes.'

As his mouth sought hers eagerly she realised she had to think fast or she would never have time to think at all. Alex's hand was already sliding along her thigh inside her nightdress and she could hear the heavy thud of his heart as he kissed her deeply. Her mind closed, cold and clear, shutting out the press of urgent desire in her body. She twisted her head away and said in a cool voice: 'First, we make terms.'

Alex stiffened on top of her. There was a brief pause, then his head lifted. She felt the shaft of the grey eyes. 'Well?' he asked tersely.

'What are you offering me?' She knew one thing he was offering her. Try as she could she had found it almost irresistible, the experienced caressing movements of his long hands, the demanding pressure of his powerful body on her. That pressure lifted now.

Alex had sat up. He was looking at her expressionlessly. 'I told you my offer once before.'

'An apartment in New York,' Sophie said as though considering it.

'If that's what you want. I want you in New York so that I can see you as often as possible. I'm more often in the States than anywhere else.' He was talking curtly, his voice rough.

She sat up carefully, slid herself round to sit beside him on the couch, being wary not to arouse his suspicions, moving close to him so that her body touched his in apparent relaxation.

'What else?'

She caught the flash of sheer rage in his eyes. 'What else do you want, you greedy little bitch?' Alex's voice shook as he asked that. 'I told you, you can have whatever you want. You won't find me lacking in generosity.'

'A car,' Sophie said softly.

He made a grimacing gesture. 'Yes, yes, whatever you want.' His mouth twisted in an ugly little sneer. 'What were you hoping to screw out of me? Not marriage, for God's sake? How high did you think I'd go?'

Sophie threw him a poised and casual smile. 'I thought Greeks believed in bargaining before they sold.'

She almost thought he flinched, then his eyes ran over her in a contemptuous, harsh glance of anticipated possession. 'I hope you're going to be worth it.' She sensed that he was about to take her in his arms again and smiled at him sweetly, her eyes not quite unveiled, her lashes flickering.

'Can we have a drink to seal the bargain?'

He glanced round, saw the decanter and got up to pour some whisky. Sophie was at the door before he even realised she had moved. She heard his swift movement, caught the steel of the grey eyes, but she had already opened the door and fled through it as Alex came after her. Sophie was sleeping next to his mother's room. She knew he would not dare to make a scene so close to his mother. Even so, he caught up with her as she reached her room. His hand wrenched at her wrist and she turned on him, saying loudly: 'Goodnight, Mr Lefkas.'

'What the hell are you playing at?' he hissed, keeping his voice down. 'What new game is this?'

Sophie lifted angry eyes to him. 'No games, Mr Lefkas. For the last time, the answer is no. I'm not interested. You can't buy me. You can't seduce me—no, no, no! Do you want me to shout it so that everyone can hear?'

He stared at her, the strong, hard face convulsed with rage. 'What do you mean, no? Just now you were going crazy in my arms. You wanted me as much as I wanted you.' His grey eyes held a molten frustration, his voice was unsteady. 'You can't walk out on me now. If you're waiting for me to raise the price, forget it.'

'Price?' Sophie spat the word back, her own face now torn with anger. 'You put a price on everything and know the value of nothing, don't you? I'm not for sale!'

'Then why did you bargain with me?' He stared at her, his lips curling in an ugly little sneer. 'What didn't I offer you that you wanted, I wonder? Or can I guess? What sort of fool do you take me for? I'm not that desperate for you.'

Sophie looked at him in bewilderment, wondering what he was talking about, but before he had time to say any more his mother's door opened and Alex stiffened, his face flushing even deeper.

'Alex!' Madame stared hard at them both, taking in Sophie's flushed dishevelled state. Sophie mumbled something incoherent, clutched her negligee around her, and retreated hurriedly into her own room. Madame demanded, 'Alex, what's going on? Why were you shouting at Sophie? What have you been up to?'

'Oh, hell and damnation!' Alex muttered savagely. Sophie stood, listening to his rapid movements as he walked away. A door slammed. Madame sighed and after a moment went back into her own room.

Sophie stood in the darkness, trembling, her face filled with distaste for herself and for Alex Lefkas.

She was appalled at what had happened. She had never behaved like that in her life, lost to all common sense and reason, letting a man she did not even like use her body with passion and desire, so that she had come very close to the brink of absolute surrender to him.

She could not actually believe what happened had happened to *her*. She couldn't even comfort herself by pretending Alex Lefkas had forced her to permit his caresses. She had wanted them. She had been as responsive as any man could expect of a woman in love, yet she had no feelings for Alex Lefkas, or at least none that had any shadow of feeling in them.

His way of life, his attitudes, his hard arrogance, his amorality, all repelled her. Yet she had ached for a few moments to give her body to him. She had kissed him passionately, trembled at the hunger she could feel inside him.

She knew, of course, why she had responded like that. In a strange way, his passion had been a safe substitute for the passion she really wanted. She could never let her desire for the man she loved blossom into fruition, but she was human. She felt the same drive to fulfilment every woman feels, the frailty of flesh was her own inheritance as much as that of other women. She ached to surrender her body, to let the normal sexual drive consume and complete her.

Getting into bed, she shivered in the numb chillness taking over her flesh. Sick, miserable, crumbling at last into tears, she heard the quiet telling of the hours from the clocks in the silent rooms around her.

She finally slept so close to dawn that she could already see the lightening of the London skyline as it crept closer. When she woke up she looked at the clock and was horrified to see what time it was, her eyes widening. Scrambling out of bed, she fled into the shower and quickly sluiced her fevered body before drying herself and dressing.

There was no sign of Madame. Vinny looked at her oddly as she made fresh coffee, poured her a glass of freshly squeezed orange juice and offered her toast which Sophie refused politely. 'Didn't you sleep?'

'Not very well,' Sophie admitted. 'Where's Madame?'

'Gone shopping. She left a message for you. You are to have the day off and do whatever you like.' Vinny looked at the large smug face of the kitchen clock as it silently registered the time, the electronic movement of the big black hands infinitesimal. 'What day there is left,' she added drily.

Sophie had put on a pale blue denim suit she had bought in Athens. Walking towards the front door of the flat, she found herself faced by Alex, and paled at the sight of him.

'Come in here,' he said tersely, pointing to the room he had just left.

She hesitated, biting her lower lip.

'You're quite safe from rape,' he said icily. 'Vinny is within earshot if you scream.' His mouth twisted. 'Or wouldn't you scream? Maybe that's what turns you on—I hadn't thought of that.'

She walked angrily past him into a large sunny office. He sat down behind a desk, his hands flat on it, staring at them.

'We've got nothing to talk about,' Sophie said. 'I made my views clear to you last night.'

'Nothing about last night is clear,' said Alex, his black head bent. 'One minute I thought we had come to an agreement; the next you were running out on me. Why?'

Sophie moved to the window and looked out on the grey London roofs sparkling in the midday sunshine. 'Last night I think I had jet lag. I was very tired and I'd drunk several glasses of wine at supper. I apologise if I gave you the wrong impression.'

'Why did you bargain with me if you didn't intend to make a deal?' Alex asked harshly.

'It was the only way I could think of to get out of that room,' she said on a smothered sob of grim laughter. 'Not very clever, but I was in no state to think clearly.'

She heard him shift in his chair, his body moving to face her. 'I'll look after you, Sophie,' he said in a low, deep voice. 'I promise. My lawyers will draw up a private contract settling an income on you.'

'Don't!' she said fiercely.

'I can't marry you,' he burst out, taking her entirely by surprise.

Sophie looked round, her face startled. 'I didn't ask you to.'

His face was drawn, his eyes glittering. 'It's what you're waiting for, isn't it? You've got to see it from my side, Sophie. The family expect me to marry a Greek girl of good family, someone suitable, someone they all know. There are two choices open to me—both well-connected girls. Mama will probably decide which is the one.' He saw her scornful glance and added: 'It's expected of me, Sophie, listen to me. . .'

'I've listened to everything I'm going to listen to,' Sophie said icily. 'Don't you have any idea at all how insulting you are? I won't be bought. I'm a woman, not a possible possession.'

'I'm very well aware that you're a woman,' he said huskily, getting up and moving into her path as she walked away. His hand touched her arm tentatively. 'Sophie, last night. . .'

'Don't talk about it. I just want to forget it.' Her skin was burning with shame and embarrassment.

'I don't,' he said deeply, his hand sliding up her arm. 'When I heard about the earthquake it wasn't just Mama I was worried about—I was afraid for you, too. When I heard your voice sounding so normal on the phone that night, cold sweat broke out on my forehead. I hadn't realised how much I was involved with you, how much I felt for you. Let me take care of you. I want to look after you, Sophie.'

Sophie blazed into white-hot rage, turning on him with contempt. 'You want to do what? Don't use euphemisms to me! What you really mean is that you want to make me one of your whores for a while until you're tired of me. What happens then? Do I get passed on to one of your executives?'

'For God's sake,' he muttered hoarsely, his face dark red. He looked at the door. 'Vinny will hear you.'

'Good,' Sophie said aggressively. 'Why not open the door? Let a little honesty into this goldfish bowl. If you think it's too shocking to be said aloud, why do you have the nerve to put it to me at all?'

'You're making it sound ugly,' he said angrily, shifting restlessly. 'It isn't like that, not with you. That isn't how I think of you.'

Sophie's eyes were fiery, fixed in burning intensity on his face, tears behind the over-brilliant irises. 'I know how you think of me. You've made that very clear, insultingly clear. You think everyone is just a commodity for you to buy and sell. I have a body you want to use and you're ready to pay handsomely so long as I don't get greedy and ask too much.' Her voice was rising, quivering.

'You're hysterical,' Alex said, his eyes anxious, his face disturbed. 'Darling . . .'

The tears spilled from her eyes. She slapped his hands away as he tried to put his arms round her.

'Don't you darling me, you phoney! I wouldn't touch you with a bargepole. It would make me sick to my stomach to have you lay a finger on me now!'

She ran past him, sobbing, and stumbled out of the door. Alex stood staring after her.

CHAPTER FIVE

SHE spent the day in London, feeling strangely distraught and on the point of tears all day. For so long she had lived in an emotional vacuum, existing with a memory which acted like a drug, trapping her with it and making her so addicted that she did not even want to get free. No man had ever got through the barriers Sophie had placed around herself; she had never been either physically or emotionally drawn to anyone else. Despite the pain she had suffered, she felt oddly calm, withdrawn to a point of balance where she could contrive to exist somehow apart from life, on a mental desert island alone with her addictive memory.

Last night and then again this morning, Alex Lefkas had somehow broken through her shielding barriers.

It had not been an emotional contact. It had been purely physical, a reflex response of the body which the mind had been unable to control and with which the heart had had no contact.

She despised him for what he had said to her. Planning to marry so coldbloodedly, choosing between two women as though they were toys he meant to purchase, talking about her, herself, as though she were up for auction to the highest bidder.

Was that really how he saw her?

Yes, she thought, pausing in front of the plate-glass windows of one of the great London stores, staring absently at a thin girl in black jeans and a cotton T-shirt who was adjusting the hang of a garment. The girl looked round and gestured, asking in mime if the dress looked okay. Staring, Sophie was blank for a second, then, understanding, smiled and nodded.

Moving on, her thoughts broken, she gave a deep sigh. How dare he crudely offer to buy her like that? Who did he think he was? What did he think she was?

As if she didn't know the answer to that! He honestly believed, apparently, that she was just holding out for some price he hadn't yet reached. He suspected she was hoping he would be eager enough to marry her.

She shuddered. Marry Alex Lefkas? Only a blind idiot would be dumb enough. He'd deceive you left and right with other women. He would neglect you, order you around, treat you as a possession rather than a person.

She shook free of her thoughts, pushing him out of her mind. For an hour she concentrated on the shopping she intended to buy, choosing some light cotton dresses and some new shirts, some sandals and some new underwear.

What had happened between her and Alex Lefkas had distressed her at some level she could not reach with conscious thought. Although she told herself she disliked and despised him, she felt oppressed and miserable as she wandered around. It was not pleasant to be regarded as an object.

She was reluctant to go back to the apartment. When she did, however, to her relief Alex was out. Madame asked her if she had enjoyed her day in London. Sophie lied and smiled and said she had. Madame looked at her thoughtfully.

'What was going on last night, Sophie?'

As calmly as she could, Sophie lied again. 'Nothing, Madame. A slight dispute between your son and myself.'

Madame watched her, the dark eyes vivid in the lined thin face. The silvery white hairs among her black hair sparkled in the lamplight.

'Slight? Alex was almost manic!'

Sophie flushed. 'I'd rather you asked him, Madame.'

'I see,' Madame said slowly.

Their eyes met and Sophie looked away, flushing. Yes, perhaps Madame did see. She knew her son. She had known him all his life and she must have learnt more about him than Alex would wish to admit. Madame read the gossip about his women in the papers; she had sometimes talked about it to Sophie. There had been a French actress who had cracked up after Alex dropped her. The newspapers splashed the story when she took an overdose of drugs. She had not died and Madame had shrugged, saying, 'Trying to bring him back, poor girl. All that will do is embarrass him.' Yes, Madame knew him.

'Sophie, while you are in England, you must visit your family,' she said. 'Go tomorrow, stay as long as you like. You should have a holiday. When I am ready to return to Crete I'll get in touch with you.'

Sophie felt cold and sick with excitement and alarm. She nodded. Madame would demand to know her reasons if she refused to go. She had no choice. And now that her mind had been made up for her, she was taut with anticipation, half afraid, half ecstatic.

She knew, of course, why Madame was sending her away home. Madame was being kind and thoughtful. Sophie smiled at her brightly, her eyes too wide and brilliant, excitement running like flame over her skin. Madame stared at her intently.

'Are you in love with Alex, Sophie?' she asked so suddenly that Sophie involuntarily gave her a totally honest answer by reflex, beginning to laugh.

'No, Madame, not even a fraction in love.'

Madame looked gravely at her, the dark eyes oddly sad. 'I see,' she said on a dull intonation.

Alex did not appear that evening while Sophie and Madame were up. Sophie went to bed early to make up for all the sleep she had lost last night. She woke up equally early, packed and said goodbye to Madame, leaving her the address of her parents.

Madame kissed her, held her close for a moment. 'Look after yourself, Sophie.'

'And you,' said Sophie, half scolding, totally affectionate. 'Have a wonderful time in London.'

On the way to the station she sat on the edge of her seat staring out at the busy London streets—people rushing to work, taxis swerving in and out of lines of traffic, the smell of petrol fumes and the sound of throbbing engines, all so familiar to her once and so very unfamiliar now.

Charing Cross was packed, but the traffic was all coming into London, little of it going the other way. As they drew out of the dirty, smoky station she gazed out at the sticky suburbs of London flashing past, aching to see the green fields of Kent once more.

She had not been home for so long. Her letters had all been brief functional records of her job, little descriptions of Crete sandwiched between the dull details of her daily life. She had rung her mother last night, surprising and delighting her with the news that she was coming home, but her mother had just been off to a meeting of a local women's club and Sophie hadn't lingered to talk of anything. They would have plenty of time to talk, her mother had said excitedly.

Except that there was nothing Sophie could talk about to her mother. She had lived with this hidden passion for five years, but it had got no easier to lie to her parents, to deceive and pretend. She hated the necessity to hide things from them, even feelings. She had often longed to be free to let the whole world see how she felt, but it was impossible for so many reasons.

Deception, she had found, became a way of life and involved far more than one at first realised. It was not merely that one had to clamp a mask over one's face. People would ask point-blank: 'Have you ever been in love?' Or say coyly: 'One day Mr Right will come along for you, Sophie,' apparently quite unaware of any wound they might inflict or insolence they might be offering. One learnt to smile, to shrug, to pretend. It was distasteful and depressing.

The familiar sights of Kent surrounded her. She sat and looked out at the cowled oasthouses, the hedge-rimmed fields, the elms and oaks which made a deep shadow for cows to graze in, and the serried ranks of hops or lines of apple trees.

When her taxi deposited her at her home she almost stumbled to the door, hoping her wary anxiety would not be visible, praying that her parents would be there alone.

She was in luck. Hugged, exclaimed over, told how brown she was, kissed and enthused over, she was pulled into the house between her parents. Sophie loved them dearly and knew they loved her. She hated spending so much time away from them. She hated what they must believe to be her indifference to them.

'You're so elegant!' her mother exclaimed, half envious.

'What's it like moving among the rich?' her father asked, laughing, quite amused at the idea of his daughter in that company.

'What is Madame Lefkas really like?'

'Is Alex Lefkas the Lothario the papers say he is?' Her father, puffing on his pipe, twinkled at her as he asked that and Sophie smiled drily back at him.

'Madame is a darling and yes, Alex Lefkas is Don Juan in person.'

Her mother eyed her. 'Attractive, darling?'

Sophie wasn't fooled by the mild face. 'Not to me, Mum.'

Her father chuckled. 'She's been torn between fretting in case he seduces you and imagining herself as his mother-in-law.'

'I have not,' her mother protested, laughing. 'What lies!'

'How is everyone?' Sophie asked casually, glancing over the room which looked so small and cramped to her after the spacious rooms at the villa.

'Fine,' her father said as casually. 'Patsy is doing a holiday job between terms at the university. She'll be home soon.'

'Aunt Daphne had an operation on her toe,' her mother said.

'Is she all right now?' Sophie dared not ask the question hovering on her lips, waiting for the name to come up naturally. She had not spoken to him for months. She had not seen him, heard more than a passing reference to him. She waited, aching to hear them say his name.

'Mary had her baby,' her father said.

'A girl,' said her mother. 'Pretty little thing, but it has George's long nose, I'm afraid.'

Sophie laughed, hoping it sounded natural. 'How is George?'

'Fine,' her father said. His face sobered. 'Elaine has just come out. Simon hopes this time she may be cured, but I warned him not to hope for too much. Lucy is at a new school. They hope it may work wonders for her. Oh, did I tell you, Gerard bought a new car and crashed it the very first day he drove it?'

Very pale, Sophie asked, 'Was he hurt?' The stiff

movement of her lips blurred the words, but her parents didn't seem to notice.

'A broken arm and a couple of ribs bust,' her father said drily. 'Gerard's the worst driver I ever met. His insurance must be colossal.'

'Kate ought to do the driving for him,' her mother said, clicking her tongue.

'How is Kate?' Sophie asked.

'You know Kate,' they said together, and then laughed.

'Yes,' said Sophie, getting up. 'Can I unpack? I want to look at my room. I hardly remember it, I've been away so long.'

'Too long,' her father said bluntly, and her mother looked at him, shaking her head.

Sophie went out and later stood at her bedroom window staring up the broad green sweep of the hill at Dancing Court, mesmerised as always by the sheer impact of the house, her eye slowly tracing the pure white line of the façade, with its classical lines unmarred by any alteration since the day it was built in the middle of the eighteenth century. Sunlight glittered back at her from the flat sash windows. The elms and oaks surrounding it left dark pools of liquid shadow on the gravel paths intersecting the carefully landscaped garden. Dancing Court was trapped for ever in a spell of idyllic grace which the summer afternoon enhanced and gilded.

Far away the green fields and woods swept into the distant weald of Kent to the south and to the north ran down to the chalk downlands bordering the English channel.

A speckled mistlethrush perched on a branch and sang distrustfully, turning his glittering eye in a semi-circle to watch for predators, listening all the time for the worms tunnelling under the grass.

Turning away, Sophie's eye was caught by a dress she

had unpacked a moment earlier. It hung on the rail of her wardrobe, the folds slightly crushed.

It was far and away the prettiest dress she had ever owned. Madame had chosen it, despite Sophie's amazed protest at the incredible price. Sophie had not yet worn it. It had been absurd to pack it for this visit and she had sheered away from any admission as to why she had brought it.

Dangerous, she thought, grimacing wryly. It was dangerous even to think of wearing it when she saw him. It would be asking for trouble to go near him in a dress like that.

Then she imagined the look in his eyes when he saw her in it, and her lids closed tightly, a grim look around her mouth. Oh, God, it would be worth it, even for a moment, to have him look at her with passion and hunger.

She bit her lower lip until it bled. She would not, must not think like that. Why did she find it so impossible to escape from him? Spinning round and round eternally in a helpless vortex from which she would give anything to break free, and yet into which one look from him could pull her in a drowning, despairing weakness?

I've tried, she told herself, staring at her own face in the mirror. I've stayed away for months, banished his memory from my mind, and even thought at times I'd been successful, only to have him spring out again like a genie from a bottle, invading my thoughts whenever I removed the clamp on them.

It was useless. Love couldn't be killed when it was so strong. It burnt and ached inside one night and day, despite the starvation imposed on it by the will, despite all that the mind can do to kill it.

A tap at the door made her stiffen, her face forced into a bright social mask. 'Come in.'

Her sister poked her head round the door, laughing, her round freckled face sunburnt, her hazel eyes lively.

'Patsy!'

Patsy hugged her and Sophie stood back to survey her younger sister. Patsy had grown up in the past year, she thought. She was a small, tightly built girl with thick brown curls and eyes like their father, sensible, kind and loving eyes, faintly myopic when she wasn't wearing the spectacles she needed for looking at the television.

'I almost feel I should curtsey,' Patsy mocked.

Sophie laughed, 'Don't be absurd!'

'Imagine you living with one of your original tycoon-playboys!'

Sophie wondered drily what Patsy would say if she knew how close those words had come to being the strict truth. If Alex Lefkas had his way she would become his mistress, and that fact could not long have been concealed from her family. Sophie wasn't innocent of the consequences which would follow if she had in fact accepted Alex's proposals. Gossip would spread from family friends to the newspapers. Her family would be shattered, shocked, ashamed.

Smiling at Patsy, she corrected her, 'With his mother, actually, to be strictly accurate.'

'Oh, come on, he must pop in to see his mum,' said Patsy, grinning.

'Very occasionally,' Sophie said. 'New York is a long way from Crete. He doesn't pop in for tea, if that's what you meant.'

'Don't disillusion me,' Patsy retorted. 'All my college friends are agog with envy. I'm famous as the girl whose sister lives with Alex Lefkas. I'm hoping to go back next term with some straight-from-the-horse's-mouth facts. So come on, is he as good-looking as his pictures?'

'I suppose he's good-looking,' Sophie shrugged.

'You don't fool me,' Patsy protested. 'All this casual indifference can't be genuine. I bet he's a sexy beast with charm coming out of every pore.'

'Out of every banknote, more likely,' Sophie snapped in sudden savagery, and caught her sister's look of astonishment. She laughed hurriedly. 'I barely know him,' she went on huskily. 'He's only been to Crete a couple of times since I went there. And once he had a party of friends with him.'

'Anyone famous?' asked Patsy avidly.

'I'd never heard of them.'

'Oh, you!' Patsy sighed in disgust. 'You're no fun. How can you live with someone as sexy as that and be so boring about him? How about his women? Met any of them?'

'One,' said Sophie. 'She was head over heels, but I don't think he gave a damn.' Not a damn, she thought flatly. Alex had made love to Patrice Lerrand, flirted with her, and Sophie suspected it had all been a goad for *her*. Alex had kissed Patrice under her window to make her jealous. He had brought the girl there deliberately just for that reason. It hadn't occurred to her at the time. Now she knew him better and she distrusted everything he said, everything he did.

'It's incredible,' Patsy went on, 'the way you fell into that job! Is it exciting, Sophie? Working for the Lefkas family?'

'Madame is a darling,' Sophie told her, smiling. 'She really is—one of the nicest people I've ever met.'

Eyeing her, Patsy said: 'But you wouldn't rave about him? Is that it?'

'Not precisely,' Sophie agreed, her eyes rueful.

'Not as glamorous as the papers make him, then?'

'He works a lot harder than they imagine and he's a lot tougher,' said Sophie.

'Oh, damn!' grinned Patsy. 'And I was imagining you being set up with your own apartment and a diamond necklace!'

Sophie's face showed a startled shock for a second and her sister looked hard at her, her own face reflecting curiosity.

Pulling herself together, Sophie said lightly: 'I'm not the type.' Her darkened lashes flicked down. The faint flush on her cheekbones might have been mere excitement at being home.

'It's wonderful to have you here,' said Patsy, leaning back, her hands on the bed as she lounged on it. 'Mum and Dad miss you. You ought to come home more often.'

Sophie heard the faint questioning in her sister's voice, but she ignored it. 'I try to write as often as I can.'

'They love getting your letters, especially since you started working for the Lefkas family. Mum's fascinated by them. It's given her new status with the neighbours, although she's got some snide hints that your job involves being available for Alex Lefkas now and then.'

'You're beginning to make me feel almost guilty because it isn't true,' Sophie said in mock regret.

Patsy laughed and got up. 'Coming down?'

'Yes,' said Sophie, joining her. 'I need a holiday. Did I tell you about the earthquake?'

'Mum said something,' Patsy nodded. 'What happened?'

Sophie hoped that Patsy's curiosity about Alex was now satisfied and she wouldn't have to fend off any further probes about him, but she found she was mistaken. He seemed to fascinate everyone she met. People barely waited to say hello to her in the street without asking avidly what Alex Lefkas was really like and watching her intently as though dying to ask pointblank if she was sleeping with him. Some of her relatives made jokes about it, but under their light tones was a devouring curiosity. The image of the glamorous playboy clung to Alex here as elsewhere. Sophie was sick of the sound of his name within three days.

The weather had continued hot and sultry. She lounged in the garden staring up at Dancing Court, watching the glint of the windows and wondering if she should walk up to make polite enquiries about Elaine. She had not seen the family at Dancing Court since she arrived. They were distant relatives whose contact with the Bryants was at a minimum, although Mrs Bryant was very proud of the connection. Elaine was Sophie's second cousin. Her marriage to the owner of the house had been an exciting event to Mrs Bryant, who had never been inside Dancing Court until the wedding. Sophie smiled over her mother's little social ambitions, tolerant of them because her affection made them unimportant.

Closing her eyes, she shivered, despite the heat. She had caught sight of the man she loved the day before—driving past her at a ferocious speed, his head tilted so that she could only catch his profile. He had not seen her, she knew, but that one brief glimpse of him had made her heart turn over. She needed to see him, talk to him. Oddly, Alex Lefkas had intensified that need, his lovemaking arousing her to feelings she had suppressed for years. The image she had carried in her heart was not fading, but she felt she had to renew it, as though the possibility of it fading had just occurred to her. The intense sexual demand Alex had made on her had shown up the emptiness of her long passion.

Lifting her head, she listened as the doorbell rang in the house. A sigh came from her. Her family were all out. She had hoped to have an hour of peace. She went into the house and wandered to the door. As it opened and she saw who was standing there, her lips parted on an audible gasp of disbelief.

'What do you want?'

Alex Lefkas put his hand on the doorframe, leaning there, as though to stop her closing the door on him again. 'I had to drive my mother down to Tonbridge to stay with an old school friend, so I thought I'd call in to see you on my way back.'

Sophie's brows shot up. 'Tonbridge isn't anywhere near here.'

'Don't argue with me, Sophie,' Alex said drily. 'All right, I wanted to see you.'

Her face ran with colour. 'I don't want to get into one of those discussions again, please. Just go away!'

'Can't I meet your family?' He was looking at her through the black lashes, his grey eyes gleaming, that hard mouth of his curling up in a far too charming smile.

She shook her head, trying to bar his entry. 'I'd rather you just left, Mr Lefkas.'

'How can you keep calling me that?' he asked with a wry little grimace. 'We got past all that long ago.' His glance slid from her fiery bright curls to the white sandals on her feet, taking their time to admire her slender body in the silky blue shift which was so simply cut that it deceived one into imagining that it was inexpensive, yet which had such a deceptive elegance and flattered every line of her figure.

'You look lovely, Sophie. You have charming taste. Everything you wear looks as though it was invented just for you.'

He was flattering her assiduously, Sophie thought, but why? Surely he hadn't come down here to her family home in the hope of bringing more pressure to bear on her to become his mistress?

'Please go,' she muttered, looking away because the intent brightness of his eyes made her nervous. For months the way Alex Lefkas looked at her had been getting under her skin. Try as she might, she couldn't ignore those teasing grey eyes.

He suddenly took her by the waist and as she gasped in angry protest, lifted her out of the way, smiling down at her with his brows quivering in amusement as he put her down again.

'Get out!' Sophie burst out.

He closed the door and leaned on it. 'Introduce me to your parents.'

'They're out,' she admitted reluctantly, then gave him an angry look. 'That doesn't mean ...'

He lifted a finely shaped hand, silencing her with a finger laid on her mouth. 'I haven't come here to repeat my offer, Sophie.'

Her colour was vivid, her eyes angry. 'Why have you come?'

'I hated it when you started to cry,' he said deeply, his face very serious, looking down at her with a light in the grey eyes which took her by surprise. 'Hated it, Sophie. You made me feel a heel.'

'Aren't you?' She said that with fierce emphasis and was pleased to see the dark red invading his face.

He nodded, his mouth straight. 'I deserve that, although I've never been called one before—or a phoney. That was a punch below the belt. You held up a mirror and showed me a face I'd never seen before. I didn't like it much.'

'Neither do I,' Sophie muttered.

'No.' He grimaced. 'I'm sorry, Sophie. That's why I'm here—I came to apologise, make my peace with you. I behaved like a swine, but past experience with women had taught me that everyone has their price.'

'Your experience is very limited, then,' she said under her breath.

Alex gave her a strange, wry look, his grey eyes almost

melancholy. 'Rather wider than yours, I'm afraid. I've learnt that you can buy most things and most people. The world is full of beautiful women happy to exchange their favours for the good things of life.'

'I'm not one of them,' said Sophie, her head bent.

'No,' he said on a strange husky note. 'I'll be honest. I'd hoped you were.'

Sophie turned away, her face burning. 'Don't say any more.'

'You're so very lovely,' Alex said behind her in that deep, warm voice, a faint unsteadiness in it.

'Don't start again,' Sophie muttered in a tight, angry voice, swinging back to face him with her hands clenched at her sides.

'I'm just making excuses for myself,' he said drily, shaking his head. 'I know my reputation probably gives you the impression I keep some sort of harem but, to be frank, I wouldn't have either the time or the energy. My relationships have usually been on a rather less glamorous basis. I've had mistresses in the past, several of them, and I've had the occasional affair, but I work too hard to be the playboy the press believe I am.'

'I don't want to hear the details of your private life,' Sophie said icily, peculiarly angry with him, looking away from his intent face.

'I want to tell you,' said Alex, watching her. 'I like women, I won't pretend I don't, and I've always managed to get those I fancied.'

'Be quiet!' Sophie said on a fierce note, her green eyes flaring at him.

Alex's eyes brightened. 'Don't be angry, Sophie,' he whispered, touching her arm with one hand. 'It isn't something I'm particularly proud of, but it's the truth and I want you to hear me admit it. I'm a man with a strong sex drive. I enjoy women's company and I like making love to them. Mostly, they seem to like it, too, and they certainly like my money. The usual arrangement works very well.'

'I'm sure it does,' Sophie muttered. 'I don't want to know. Get out of here and leave me alone!'

'How was I to know you were different?' he asked, his hand stroking her arm.

She pulled her arm away. 'I told you so.'

'I thought it was part of the usual ritual,' Alex said drily. 'It may interest you to know, by the way, that I got it in the neck from Mama after you'd gone. She had guessed I'd made some sort of pass and she was furious with me. She said if you left her because of me, she'd give me hell.'

Sophie's face softened and she smiled. 'I love your mother.'

'I know.' Alex met her eyes and his smile was warm. 'So do I, very much.'

She nodded, her eyes vivid. 'I realise that.' It was his most attractive quality, that tender caring for his mother. Over the months she had known him, it had impressed her. He was in constant contact, wherever he was in the world, making sure his mother was safe and happy.

'It's one thing we have in common,' Alex said.

'The only thing!'

He shook his head decisively. 'Don't lie, Sophie.'

'Lie?' She looked at him, her face running with colour.

'It wasn't just me going crazy that night.' His voice was deepening, warming, an intimate husky note in it. The grey eyes gleamed through their black lashes as Sophie looked hurriedly away, biting her lip.

'That's why I'm here,' Alex said, moving closer. 'You made me admit what I think I've known for a long time. This time it's different, and you know it as well as I do. I was trying to pretend it wasn't because it shook me rigid even to consider the alternative, but you've forced me to take a good, hard look at myself.'

What was he talking about? Sophie thought, her face bemused. He was talking in riddles.

His hand lifted to touch her cheek tenderly. 'My mother said I was the base Indian who threw away a pearl worth more than his whole tribe, and she's absolutely right. I'm not imagining things, am I, Sophie? You were trembling in my arms that night. You came very close to giving me what I wanted so badly.'

'No,' she moaned, horrified.

'Don't lie to me, Sophie, not now,' he said unsteadily, caressing her face.

'What are you talking about?' Sophie could not meet the serious, intent stare.

'You know very well what I'm talking about,' Alex told her with a faint smile.

She shook her head feverishly.

'You wanted me that night. The response was blazing out of you. It nearly drove me out of my mind. Are you a virgin, Sophie? Did I scare you? Although you were responding I got the strongest feeling it was the first time for you. I couldn't believe it, but it made me almost ill with pleasure.'

'Stop it! You said you wouldn't start again, you said you came to apologise, and all the time it was just another approach ...' Sophie looked at him with all her anger and distaste flashing in her eyes.

'No,' Alex broke in huskily, shaking his head. 'Don't you understand what I'm saying? Oh, Sophie ...'

The door bell rang in a peremptory fashion and he broke off, swearing under his breath. Trembling, flushed, Sophie turned on a reflex action to open the door, and then stood staring in wide-eyed shock at the woman who stood outside.

'Whose is the chariot, darling?' Elaine Harcourt threw a glance over her shoulder at the long silver limousine standing outside. 'Don't tell me you own it? Are you too important to use trains these days? Or was it a payment for services rendered to your notorious employer?'

Elaine had a smoky, soft voice with a permanent thread of malice running through it, especially when she spoke to Sophie, and the tone and words brought Sophie's colour burning back into the face which had paled at the sight of Elaine.

Alex moved abruptly and Elaine glanced past Sophie, her eyebrows lifting in amused surprise.

'Oh, dear,' she purred, unabashed at the sight of him. 'Have I put my foot in it?'

Sophie felt ill as she watched the catlike sensuality entering Elaine's face. She knew that look—Elaine in sight of prey, acquisitive, predatory, her body rippling with all too explicit invitation.

'Aren't you going to introduce us, Sophie?' As she spoke, Elaine extended her hand and Alex moved slowly forward to take it.

There was a change in him, too. Sophie watched his manner alter, his grey eyes glint.

Elaine was staggeringly beautiful, at first sight, of course. Tall, with dark red hair in a full cloudy mass around her lovely face, she had the rich, voluptuous figure of a courtesan, the low-cut summer dress she wore emphasising those curves, her breasts visible, their deep pale cleft inviting Alex's eyes as he stood close to her.

'Elaine, this is Alex Lefkas. Mr Lefkas, my cousin Elaine Harcourt.'

'How do you do?' Alex said smoothly.

Still holding his hand, Elaine gave him a languid smile. 'Have you come to take Sophie away again already? I was calling to invite her to my birthday party

tonight. I only heard she was back last night and of
course I was hoping to have a long cosy chat with her.'
The dark eyes held languorous amusement as Elaine met
Alex's eyes. Although she did not say so, she was silently
confessing that the chat would have been about him, and
Alex's wry cynical smile in return mocked her confession.

'Oh, Sophie will be here for your birthday party,' Alex
said lightly. 'I only called in to tell her something.'

Elaine's eyes widened, flicked to Sophie's still, cool
face. Alex shouldn't have said that, Sophie thought.
Elaine wasn't stupid. Alex could have phoned or written.
The fact that he came himself was far too revealing.

'Well, I'm delighted to hear that,' Elaine said softly.
'All Sophie's old flames will be eager to see her again.
Won't they, Sophie?'

Alex's dark head swung and his grey eyes fixed on
Sophie's pale face. She felt the sharp pierce of his stare.

'Sophie's a very unusual girl,' Elaine went on in the
purring voice she always used when she was thrusting
her little daggers into someone. 'She has this incredible
capacity to retain a lover even when he never sees her
from one year to the next. Still waters run deep, don't
they say? What is the secret, Sophie? What magic do
you use?'

Sophie had learnt to smile away these attacks. It was
harder than ever under Alex's hard, intent eyes. He
couldn't fail to pick up the vicious personal hostility
under Elaine's smile and soft voice.

A car horn sounded outside and Elaine gave a wry
little shrug. 'Gerard getting impatient.' Sophie stiffened
and Elaine gave her a feline smile. 'He's driving me to
Canterbury to do some shopping. I hope I get there in
one piece—but you know Gerard.' She moved to the
door. 'Shall I give him your love, Sophie?'

'Do,' Sophie said icily.

Elaine laughed, about to go, then paused and gave Alex a quick look. 'The invitation to Sophie includes you, of course, Mr Lefkas. If you just happen to be around tonight.'

The door slammed behind her. Alex watched Sophie. She fought not to let him see the shaking in her body which the tension of listening to Elaine had left, but she knew he was staring with fixed, sharp eyes.

'What was all that about?' he demanded after a pause.

She laughed rather falsely. 'Oh, just Elaine being herself.'

'Don't lie to me. She hates your guts. What was all that about a lover?'

Sophie turned away, her lips trembling.

He caught her arm and held her towards him, bending to look at her angrily. 'Sophie, look at me.'

Slowly she raised her green eyes, their colour deepened by the unshed tears burning to escape.

'What did she mean? What was behind all that? She was getting at you from the moment she arrived.'

'She doesn't like me,' Sophie said with an effort. 'She never has. But then Elaine doesn't much like anybody.'

'Who's Gerard?' he demanded, watching her.

'Another cousin,' Sophie said, her brow darkening. 'I hope to God he knows what he's doing. How can he do this to Kate? She's pregnant and they've only been married two years. I'd have thought Gerard had more sense than to get mixed up with Elaine.'

'Is he in love with you?' Alex asked flatly.

Sophie laughed wryly. 'Of course not.' She walked away into the sitting-room and Alex came after her.

'Are you in love with him?'

Sophie glanced at him, then pointed to a photograph on the mantelpiece. 'That,' she said, 'is Gerard.'

Alex swung his head to stare and his face relaxed as

he took in the heavy rough brown head, the cheerfully schoolboyish grin.

'You had me worried,' he said, grinning down at her.

'You mean Elaine did,' Sophie said drily. 'Which is just what she intended. Elaine loves to make trouble.'

'I'll keep an eye on her,' Alex murmured. 'Will this party be formal tonight?'

Sophie looked startled. 'You weren't thinking of going?'

'Why not? I was invited.'

'You can't,' Sophie said urgently, her hand gripping his arm. 'Alex, please, I'd rather you didn't.'

He looked at her intently. 'Will it make all your old flames jealous, Sophie?'

Her cheeks burnt. 'Elaine was being funny.'

'I wasn't amused,' said Alex. 'I didn't like the lady. I didn't like the way she looked at you or the way she talked to you. Will I do as I am or should I get hold of some evening clothes?'

'Please,' she said desperately, 'don't go.'

'Why not?' The narrowed eyes shot over her worried face. 'Why not, Sophie?'

'It would cause talk,' she muttered, looking away. 'People will gossip.'

'Let them. What time shall I pick you up?'

She felt sick with premonition and dismay, shaking her head dumbly at him.

'I'll be here at seven-thirty,' he said when she didn't answer. 'It will give me time to meet your family. I'm sure they'll be relieved to find I don't have cloven hoofs or a tail.'

CHAPTER SIX

WHEN Sophie informed her family of Alex's impending arrival, they were flung into confusion. 'No, Sophie!' her mother almost shrieked, looking round the casual untidy sitting-room. 'How could you let him see the house in this state? Did he come in here? Look at your pipes, Joe—dirty old things! Magazines on the floor, my sewing basket left open ... what must he have thought?'

Her father groaned. 'That's torn it,' he told Sophie. 'Why didn't you send him packing? She'll turn the house upside down now and we'll have no peace until he's been and gone.'

'Patsy, get the vacuum cleaner. Sophie, pick up all those magazines. Joe, get rid of those pipes and don't leave them around again. Is there any whisky? Did you buy soda, Joe, when we ran out? Or does he take ginger with it? Sophie, does he take soda or ginger?' Mrs Bryant was panic-stricken, her face flushed, her manner distracted. Sophie looked at her with wry impatience.

'Don't get flustered, Mum. Alex won't give a damn if you've got soda or ginger.'

There was an odd little silence. Patsy stood in the doorway, the vacuum cleaner in her hand. Mrs Bryant stared, open-mouthed. Mr Bryant fingered his lapel thoughtfully. Looking from one to the other, Sophie felt herself flushing, and realised that her tone had aroused their suspicions. Since she got home she had been careful to call him Mr Lefkas and to imply that she had scarcely met him. Now Alex had descended on them without warning and was actually planning to take her to a party

98

tonight, and she had compounded it by calling him Alex in that casual way in the manner of someone very much more intimately acquainted with him than she had let them believe.

'Why did he come down here, Sophie?' Her father did not look at her, still moving a hand up and down his lapel.

Sophie hesitated briefly. 'He had a message from Madame. He'd just driven her to stay with someone near here and was passing.' It sounded thin and Patsy's derisive grin told her as much.

'Is he staying with this person too?' her father asked.

'I don't know.' Sophie had no idea where Alex was staying or where he was at this moment. He had gone without telling her his plans.

'What was the message, Sophie?' Patsy asked, almost laughing in her face. 'Was it important?'

'Yes.' Sophie hoped her lie sounded convincing.

'What was it?'

'Patsy!' Mrs Bryant broke in, very flushed. 'That's none of your business.'

'It was confidential,' Sophie faltered.

'I bet,' said Patsy, eyeing her in a way Sophie found embarrassing. 'I knew all that indifference was too good to be true.'

'Patsy, go and check on the whisky,' Mrs Bryant said firmly. Patsy went, shrugging, and Mrs Bryant muttered, 'Sophie, you won't lose your head, will you? I mean, I'm sure he's very attractive, but ...'

'I'm in no danger of losing my head, I promise,' said Sophie, looking at her levelly.

'It's Sophie's business,' said Mr Bryant, collecting up his cherished pipes lovingly. 'Leave it alone, dear.'

Mrs Bryant subsided, a line around her mouth. Sophie helped her to restore the room to order and then went up to change. She hesitated in front of the dress, torn between contradictory impulses, then snatched it down with a defiance which made her green eyes flash.

Damn Elaine, she thought. Damn all of them! Some half an hour later she looked at herself in the mirror and knew she looked better than she had ever looked in her life. While she was staring at her own reflection she heard the doorbell, and her heart thudded. Alex, she thought, hurrying to the top of the stairs.

Patsy had opened the door. Alex was looking at her with one dark eyebrow arched enquiringly, the teasing little smile he could give when he wanted to charm hovering around his hard mouth. 'You must be Patsy.'

Patsy sounded breathless. 'Yes. Hallo. Won't you come in?' Sophie saw her sister shoot an enthralled look over his wide shoulder at the sleek car drawn up outside. The neighbours would be having a field day, Sophie thought drily.

She started down the stairs and Alex turned. The smile on his face went. His eyes gleamed like cool bright water as he watched her moving towards him. The green was light and springlike, a floating material with silvery threads emblazoned on the surface, moulding her body lovingly, the frilled pleated sleeves full and cape-like to the elbow.

Under the light her hair picked up fire and glittered, the soft waves tumbling round her face. The dress laid bare her gleaming tanned shoulders and the beginning of the cleft between her high breasts.

Patsy was looking from Sophie to Alex avidly, her lips parted in breathless excitement.

Alex moved forward as Sophie reached the last step. He took her hand and kissed it, raising it to his lips. 'You're enchanting,' he murmured huskily.

The excitement inside her was lighting her eyes, giving

them a wild feverish brightness.

Smiling at him, she walked into the sitting-room. Her parents got up, looking nervous and embarrassed. Sophie introduced Alex and within minutes he had put them at their ease, turning the full shaft of that charm on them, smiling, telling them about the traffic on the motorway down from London, describing a near-miss he had had with a lorry which overtook him at high speed and came far too close. His eyes moved from one to the other, he accepted the whisky and soda, said it was his first that day. 'I'm quite abstemious, aren't I, Sophie?'

Her parents looked at her quickly. Alex saw that searching glance and deliberately touched her pink cheek with one finger. 'My mother relies on your daughter, Mr Bryant. I have strict instructions from her to take good care of Sophie tonight. Mama is terrified of losing the best secretary she ever had.'

The careful phrases calmed her parents, the talk of his mother making it all sound reassuring. As Alex had intended, Sophie thought ironically.

All the same, she was grateful to him, grateful for his care to be pleasant to her family, grateful for the admiration he did not hide whenever he looked at her, grateful for the casual charm with which he was easing the atmosphere.

Alex was on his best behaviour and although she was aware of the strategies he was employing nevertheless she had been worried about the effect of his visit on her family and now she felt much better.

Glancing at his watch, he said at last: 'We should be moving, don't you think, Sophie? I've got to get back tonight.'

'Where are you staying?' her mother asked.

Alex hesitated so briefly only Sophie probably noticed. 'Near here,' he murmured.

'With your mother's friend?' Patsy asked, and Sophie saw that Patsy, at least, was not absolutely fooled by Alex.

He gave her a dry little smile. 'Sophie told you?' He put down his glass and stood up. 'Ready, Sophie?'

He had neither agreed nor disagreed to Patsy's question, but in the moments when they moved towards the door there was no chance for Patsy to press the point.

On the drive up to Dancing Court Alex laughed softly to himself. 'Your little sister is as sharp as a knife, isn't she? What had you told them?'

'Nothing,' Sophie said flatly. 'Did you think I'd boast about it? If they guessed at what had happened, they'd press me to leave your mother.'

'Then they don't know you very well,' Alex said softly. He reached across and took her hand, kissed it lightly. 'If I'd seen you looking the way you do now a few weeks ago, I'd have moved heaven and earth to get you into bed.'

'You're impossible,' Sophie protested, but couldn't help laughing at the self-mocking note in his voice.

'You can't have seen yourself in a mirror or you wouldn't be surprised,' he smiled at her. His eyes moved from her face a moment later and he whistled as he looked at the white façade of the house. 'Good lord! Who did you say owned it?'

'Elaine's husband,' Sophie said as he drew the smooth-running car to a stop.

'Elaine married into money, obviously,' said Alex with a certain cynicism. 'She looked as though that was the way her mind would work.'

'Get out your chequebook,' Sophie muttered savagely. 'She's not hard to buy.'

He swung to stare at her in open surprise. She flushed and got out of the car. Alex joined her, still narrow-eyed.

'That was said with real hatred,' he observed. 'You really don't like her, do you?'

'I ought to warn you,' Sophie said in an unsteady voice, 'Elaine drinks. And when she drinks, she's even nastier than when she's sober.'

He whistled under his breath. 'Thanks for the warning. I hadn't thought that was possible. What has she got against you, Sophie?' He watched her closely. 'What have you got against her?'

'We don't like each other much,' Sophie shrugged with conscious irony as she walked towards the front door.

She knew from the ripple of whispers which ran round the room that Elaine had already noised abroad the possibility that Alex would be here tonight. Sophie knew most of the people in the large, crowded room. Her eyes flicked round, returning smiles, and then Elaine was there, scrutinising her from head to toe with a hard glint in her eyes. 'Angel, how chic! You make me feel positively gaudy.'

Giving her a calm, careful smile Sophie said, 'You always look marvellous, Elaine.'

It was true. The clinging ivory silk gave her ripe beauty the perfect setting, her full breasts soft and rounded under the material. Diamonds glittered round her throat and on her hand. Elaine, as mistress of Dancing Court, was superb.

Smiling in that catlike fashion, her red mouth bloomed and glistening, Elaine put a hand on Alex's arm. 'Do you know, I had a feeling you would come,' she said huskily. 'What have you been doing to Sophie? She's changed beyond recognition.'

Sophie was tense and stiff, her whole face held under iron control. The man coming up behind Elaine smiled at her, catching the malice in his wife's voice.

'Don't you agree, Simon? Hasn't Sophie altered? I do

wonder what she's been doing, don't you? She looks quite out of place in this dreary little backwater of ours now—I knew those looks of hers would take her a long way if she got the chance.' It was a crude insult barely disguised by the smile and soft voice with which it was uttered. Sophie felt like slapping the smiling face. Instead she merely smiled as though it were all a great joke.

Elaine switched her smile to Alex. 'Mr Lefkas...'

'Alex,' he said, his grey eyes cynical as she paused obviously for him to do so.

She flickered her lashes at him, smiling again. 'Then you must call me Elaine. Alex, this is my husband, Simon.'

Alex shifted to offer his hand, a faint curiosity and compassion in his face as he looked at Elaine's husband.

The tall, broad-shouldered man standing beside Elaine gave him a polite smile. Under the lights his pale fair hair flittered and the blue eyes were wary, wry, sophisticated.

'Welcome to Dancing Court—any friend of Sophie's is a friend of ours.'

'Thank you,' Alex said pleasantly, noting with a shrewd eye the marks of experience and cynicism the other man's features bore, and not surprised by them with Elaine's malicious gaze on her husband. 'You have a lovely home.'

'Thank you, yes, we love it ourselves.'

'Have your family been here long?'

Simon's well-cut lips twisted. 'About five hundred years.' His voice was deep and calm, a strongly timbred voice threaded with courtesy and patience and charm, reinforced by the straight glance of his eyes. The faint weariness, the strength, which his eyes betrayed made him a man one did not forget.

Gerard came into the room and Elaine moved away towards him. Simon looked after her, his mouth wry, then looked at Sophie lightly. 'Glad to be back in England, Sophie?'

'Delighted,' she said. She glanced at Elaine and Gerard and saw the flush on Gerard's face as Elaine ran her hand up his arm. Kate, she saw, was not present; her eyes darkened.

A waiter appeared with a tray and Simon handed Sophie a glass of champagne. She sipped it and said teasingly: 'Not your best vintage, Simon?'

'I don't cast pearls,' he said, smiling lightly at her.

'Don't finish that sentence,' said Sophie, making a reproving face at him.

They laughed and Alex tilted the glass in his hand, watching the bubbles break to the surface. Sophie gave another look at Elaine and Gerard and her eyes came back to Simon. He looked drily into her eyes with a slight, ironic smile.

'How's Lucy?' she asked.

His face changed. 'Better,' he said quietly. 'We've found her a school a few miles from here and she seems to like it. She's happier. It's a hard struggle for her, poor darling, but I think she's beginning to get somewhere now.'

'I'd like to see her while I'm here.'

'Of course, come up whenever you like. You know she loves you.'

'I love her,' Sophie said, looking into his eyes.

'She'll be happy to know you haven't forgotten her with all your exciting travels. Your mother gives her the Greek stamps for her stamp collection.' Catching Alex looking at him closely, Simon turned and said coolly: 'My daughter is deaf. We've had some problems persuading her to come to terms with it.'

'How old is she?' Alex frowned, looking sober.

'Nine,' Simon said. 'She adores Sophie. Sophie is very good with her. For a long time the only person who could get Lucy to try to use the sign language was Sophie.'

'And you,' Sophie said huskily.

Simon smiled at her briefly. 'Oh, and me. But now Lucy is beginning to talk on her fingers like mad. It's very hopeful.'

Someone called him and he excused himself, walking away. Alex looked after him, his dark face grave. 'My God, poor chap. What a life! A wife who's a complete bitch and a drunk into the bargain, and a child who's deaf. No wonder he looks as if life's hell.'

'Yes,' Sophie said casually, glancing at Simon's tall back, 'Simon hasn't been too lucky.'

'That's a damned understatement,' Alex said almost as though he were really angry over Simon's misfortunes. 'He seems a decent fellow, too. If I'd had his luck I'd have drowned my sorrows, I think.'

'There's no point in having two alcoholics in one family,' Sophie said flatly.

'Does his wife drink because of the child?'

Sophie hesitated. 'Yes, I think so.'

'I don't suppose she got much joy out of it, either,' Alex commented. 'Maybe she has some excuse for being the way she is ...'

'Elaine thought when she married Simon that life would be plain sailing ever after,' Sophie said rapidly, harshly. 'When she realised Lucy was born deaf she refused to admit it. She wouldn't even touch Lucy. From the moment she was born Elaine ignored her. I think she actually hates her. She once called her deformed to me— as though her deafness was some sort of crime. Elaine can't bear the fact that a child of hers isn't perfect. She doesn't care that Lucy is an adorable child, pretty and sweet and loving. As far as Elaine's concerned, Lucy doesn't exist.'

Alex stared at her pale hard face and angry eyes. 'You care deeply about the child,' he said slowly.

'Yes,' Sophie said. 'I don't know how any mother can behave to her own child the way Elaine does to Lucy.'

'So that's why you hate her,' Alex commented.

Sophie shrugged, her excitement dwindling. 'Drink your champagne before it goes flat,' she said, tasting her own glass.

A moment later Elaine and Gerard came up to them and Sophie looked at her cousin with cold, accusing eyes. Gerard shifted his feet under her stare, coughing.

'How are you, Sophie?'

'Very well,' she said. 'How's Kate? Isn't she here to-night?'

His eyes slid away. 'Couldn't come,' he muttered. 'A bit under the weather.'

'When is the baby due?'

Gerard looked almost appealingly at her. 'Couple of months,' he said. 'It's nice to see you, Sophie.'

Elaine was leading Alex away to escort him round her guests like a captured animal, her arm on his, her face brilliant with triumph. Elaine was an ambitious woman under her silken malice. Most of her drive had gone into spite and cruelty long ago from sheer inertia because having married Simon she could climb no higher up the ladder. The house gave her cachet, conferred status on her. The money gave her all the clothes and jewellery she wanted. Elaine was bored in her role as lady of the manor; she had been for years. Now she paraded Alex as though he were a birthday present and Sophie watched her ironically, knowing from past experience that Elaine imagined she was in some way hurting her by taking Alex from her.

There was dancing later. Sophie danced with various of the men whom she knew and once or twice with Alex, but every time he came near her Elaine tried to head him off, pulling him away to talk to someone else. The room grew overheated and stuffy. Sophie was bored with polite small talk and smiles, her facial muscles stiff and weary.

She slipped around the crowded room and went out into the quiet conservatory adjoining it. The domed glass roof arched overhead, the air cool and smelling of earth. Waxen-leaved plants climbed the walls of glass. Sophie stood there, staring out at the dark night sky. Clouds massed there, moving continually across the darkness, and she watched the just visible motion with abstracted eyes.

She thought she detected the fragrance of cigar smoke and turned, but as she did so a step sounded on the marble floor.

Sophie drew a harsh breath. 'No,' she said in a low voice. 'Go back!'

The shaft of the light from the curtained windows behind him outlined the man's tall figure, his hair glittering in it.

'All alone, Sophie?' Simon pushed his hands down into the pockets of his jacket.

She clasped her hands at her waist as though they were trembling. 'Please, Simon!'

She turned and walked away from him into the dark shadows of the conservatory. A row of thick leafy ferns barred her path and just before she reached them Simon caught up with her.

From the party came the low, haunting refrain of a popular song. Simon caught her arm and spun her and Sophie looked up at him white-faced. They confronted each other like enemies, their eyes held.

'Don't,' Sophie muttered. 'Don't make me angry with you, Simon.'

'Be as angry as hell,' he said hoarsely. 'You know I've got to.'

One moment they were a pace apart, staring at each other. The next they were locked in each other's arms, their mouths moving hungrily in a kiss which went on and on, Sophie's arms round his neck, her hands running through his fair hair. Her body lay against his, pressing against him with a movement which spoke of unbearable hunger. Their mouths clung, devoured, fed so fiercely that Sophie was half suffocating as she reeled against him.

At last Simon pulled himself away as though he had to force himself to do it and looked down at her, running a trembling hand through his ruffled hair. 'God, I thought I'd go crazy, looking at you, wanting you, unable to touch you!'

She leaned back against the window, shaking. 'Simon, you shouldn't be out here. Elaine might notice.'

'She wouldn't notice if the Angel Gabriel flew down and hit her with a bottle right now,' he said savagely. 'Your friend Lefkas is all she's noticing tonight.'

Sophie winced. 'I'm sorry I brought him. She invited him and he insisted on coming.'

'Elaine's been taking great pleasure in insinuating that you're not just his mother's secretary,' Simon said, and his blue eyes held pain and jealousy as he looked at her.

Sophie looked up at him miserably. 'Oh, my darling, you know that isn't true. You didn't believe it?'

'No,' said Simon in a voice which held anguish. 'But even not believing it I've been going through hell. And just now, seeing him with you, I felt ...' He broke off, taking a thick breath. 'God knows. He's interested in you, don't tell me he isn't. Do you think I can't pick it up?

I'm too aware of you myself not to sense when another man looks at you like that.'

She flushed deeply.

Simon watched the colour sweep up her face. 'I'm right, aren't I? Elaine fancies she could get him interested in her, but I don't think he has eyes for anyone but you. I watched him. He looks at you all the time even when he's with other people. He doesn't take his eyes off you for long.'

Sophie was silent. Then she said huskily, 'You'd better go back, darling. It would be safer.'

'Not yet,' he said, his hand touching the warm smooth skin of her arm. 'Oh, God, my darling, you look like spring in that dress. Almost as lovely as you were when you were eighteen.'

She made a strange soft sound, a tormented laughter. 'Don't!'

'I dream of you and wake up feeling happy, and then it's all still there—Elaine, the drink, the emptiness. Sometimes I have this nightmare that you've married someone else and I go crazy. I smile and smile with Elaine watching me and saying things to get under my skin, and the sweat is running down my body when I wake up and some nights I'm so sick I have to walk for hours to calm myself down.'

She put her hands over her face, shuddering.

'I'm sorry, I shouldn't have told you. God, I'm a selfish swine! I swore I wouldn't say anything to make you unhappy. All I think about is myself. Sophie darling, don't cry.'

'I love you,' she moaned, and it was agonisingly sweet to say the words aloud to him.

He leaned his head on her arm, his body tense and trembling. 'My darling! If only ...'

'Don't say them, the two most painful words in the language!'

'Lucy——' he began, and she stopped him.

'Lucy matters more than we do. We know that. You can't divorce Elaine without running the risk of losing Lucy, and we know Lucy comes first. We know all that. Go away, Simon—stop tormenting me!'

He drew a rough breath, looking at her with a passion that made her whole body shake, then slowly walked away. Sophie stared after him, the hot tears rising to her eyes.

The conservatory was very quiet yet echoing with the emotions which it had held a moment ago. She leaned on the window, trying to still the beating of her heart. Suddenly a sound caught her ear. She swung, tense, and all the last vestiges of colour left her face as Alex Lefkas walked from behind the row of tall ferns at the far end of the room. In the shadows their eyes met.

'Oh, God!' Sophie breathed.

He must have heard everything; she remembered the cigar smoke she had thought she smelt.

'By the time I realised what I was hearing it was too late to come out,' Alex told her in a clipped, cool voice. 'I was in hiding from his rather too pressing wife. It seemed a quiet place to smoke a cigar. I hadn't expected to become the audience for Romeo and Juliet.' He saw the wince she gave and laughed harshly under his breath. 'It was quite a performance!'

'Don't!' she muttered, turning away to lean her white face on the window.

She heard him step closer. His voice came just behind her, the accents thickening. 'You're quite an actress. I was looking round the room all evening trying to guess if any of the men were interested in you and I didn't spot a thing. The pair of you put on a dazzling act.'

'Can't you see I don't want to talk about it?' Sophie whispered, shivering.

'I'm sure you don't,' Alex drawled icily. 'You certainly had me fooled with the cool, innocent face and the keep-your-distance patter. I was actually beginning to believe you were genuine, some sort of sleeping beauty waiting for true love.' He began to laugh without any amusement, his voice dark and savage with anger. 'I was being set up, was I?'

Sophie turned, astonished, her eyes widening.

He bent towards her, cold menace in the grey eyes. 'That was the game, wasn't it? You can't marry Romeo, so you cold-bloodedly planned to trap me, and my God! it might have worked if I hadn't been lucky enough to see the two of you together.'

Sophie's green eyes flashed, brilliant with pain and anger. 'I'd be happy if I never set eyes on you again, Mr Lefkas. Trap you? I wouldn't be seen dead with you!'

She brushed past him, moving towards the curtained windows, and he gave a snarl, dragging her back towards him, holding her shoulders in his vice-like hands, staring down at her mouth with a curious expression almost as though he could see the bruising hunger of the other man's kiss on it.

'Let go of me!' Sophie shuddered as the grey eyes lifted to meet her own.

His mouth parted on a cold sneer. 'Oh, no, not yet, you cheating little bitch.'

As his head bent towards her Sophie sobbed, 'I couldn't bear it, please, don't! Not now.'

She heard the intake of his breath, felt the tensing of his body, then his arms closed round her in a savage possession and he forced her head back under the violence of his kiss, his lips hot and angry, forcing her mouth open in a probing invasion which she could not evade. She backed, struggling, and he advanced, crushing her against the window, his body forced down against hers, the powerful thighs pulsing with desire she could feel in her own body.

'No,' she moaned under his mouth.

'Yes,' he muttered, and one hand slid down her in an intimate, fondling caress which curved around her breast, his fingers warm on the soft material.

A high, shrill laughter broke them apart. He released her and spun, his handsome face heavily flushed.

In the yellow light from the room beyond Elaine's red hair glittered like Christmas finery, the diamonds round her neck flashing. She swayed slightly, her face malicious and flushed with drink.

'My God, so it's true. Well, I'm damned! I never thought that smug little bitch had it in her. My poor darling Simon!'

Alex's eyes hardened as they moved to the man standing behind Elaine. Simon's blue stare was on Sophie, a glitter of fierce jealousy in the stunned way he was looking at her.

Sophie was frozenly, despairingly shaking her head. Her whole body was trembling.

Elaine's head swung clumsily to look round at her husband. 'Why, Simon! You've gone quite white,' she said in soft, spiteful enjoyment. 'Aren't you feeling well? You look as if you're going to throw up.'

'Shut up, you bitch!' Simon burst out rawly, the blue eyes filled with intense, despairing bitterness.

Elaine laughed, triumph in every line of her full, curved body. Simon had learnt long ago to hide his feelings from his wife's malicious eyes, but now he was betraying himself without being able to stop it, and Elaine was delighted.

Sophie bit down on her lip to stop herself crying out

against the pain in Simon's eyes. She could not bear to see that look on his face.

Turning back to Alex, who was tense and stiff, Elaine said in saccharine tones: 'Oh, you mustn't think we're shocked, Mr Lefkas—Alex. This isn't the Victorian age. Even in this boring little place we know these things happen. I'm sure you're very generous. Sophie's very lucky.'

Sophie bent her head, white, shivering, so sick she felt she might actually pass out if she didn't get away.

Alex's voice sounded at her elbow, cool and level, very polite. 'You seem to have the wrong idea, Mrs Harcourt. Sophie and I are going to be married.'

CHAPTER SEVEN

'HARD to say which of you looked the most stunned,' Alex said later with a grim smile.

'Why did you do it?' Sophie's voice was trembling as she asked. She still had not recovered from the shock of hearing him make that cool announcement.

They sat in the parked car which he had drawn up in a quiet layby some way from her home. The black night lay around them, now and then another car flashing past, headlights blazing, cutting the shadows with a yellow beam.

Alex was lighting a cigar and didn't answer for a moment, staring at the tip of it, blue smoke beginning to waft away. Taking it out of his mouth, he said flatly, 'God knows. I just wanted to wipe the smile off her face, I think.'

He had done that. Elaine had stopped laughing, envy and rage in her eyes as she stared from Sophie to Alex. Elaine had been furious at the thought of Sophie marrying the Lefkas fortune.

'But you made everything worse,' she said despairingly.

His head swung towards her, a savage smile on his face. 'For him! She was right, he did look sick. And he looked sicker after I'd said we were going to be married!'

Simon's white shock, the jealousy of his stare, came back to her.

Staring into the tangled dark hedge beside them, she said: 'I'll try to see him tomorrow, explain that it was all a joke.'

Alex exploded. 'You damned well will not!'

She stiffened, looking at him dazedly, her face tracked
with tears and pale, her green eyes puzzled. 'I've got to
tell him it isn't true!'

'No,' Alex bit out harshly.

'But I don't want him to think I lied to him, hid anything from him. What must he be feeling at this moment?
I told him there was nothing between you and me—and
then for him to see you kissing me, to be told we're going
to be married.' Her voice broke on a sob. 'Oh, God, he
must be so miserable!'

'Isn't that tough?' Alex's voice was savage and the grey
eyes had an obsidian darkness as she looked at them.

'How can you be so cruel?'

'You lied to me,' he said hoarsely. 'Now you can lie to
him.'

'I never lied to you!'

'By omission,' he snapped. 'You let me believe there
was no one in your life, that you were heartwhole, and
all the time you were nursing this furtive little hole-and-
corner affair with a married man!'

'It isn't an affair,' Sophie said, flinching, heat coming
into her white face.

His hand shot out to catch her chin, turn her face towards him. 'Lie to me this time and I think I might kill
you. Is he your lover?'

She looked at him, shivering. 'No.'

'Never?'

'No.'

The fingers tightened, biting into her jaw. 'Is that the
truth?'

Sophie wrenched her head free, her face blazing with
defiance. 'Yes, although it's no business of yours. How
dare you question me as though I were a criminal?
You've no right to demand to know anything about my

private life. Who do you think you are?'

His hard mouth twisted. 'I think I'm the man who just said he was going to marry you.'

'Don't be ridiculous,' Sophie snapped. 'That didn't mean a thing.'

'It meant this—I won't be made a fool of, and having made a statement like that in public I won't go back on it.'

'What do you mean? In public? Only Elaine and ... Simon ... heard.' Her voice broke on the second name and Alex's black head lifted sharply and turned towards her, watching the tears run down her white face. Sophie brushed them aside with a trembling hand, like a child, giving a faint forlorn sniff.

He laughed coldly. 'Do you really imagine Elaine is going to keep news like that to herself?'

Sophie stiffened, staring at him.

'Within twenty-four hours the whole damned world will know.' Alex regarded her unsmilingly, his voice level.

Sophie gasped, horrified. 'You've got to stop her—tell her it was a joke.'

'No.'

She looked at him with incredulity. 'You must!'

'Don't use the word must to me,' Alex gritted.

'Mr Lefkas,' she whispered pleadingly, 'you don't seem to realise what it will mean.'

He laughed harshly. 'Don't I?'

Sophie's head was spinning. 'Why are you being so obstinate? Are you afraid of losing face? Is that it? Oh, why did you say it? Why did you have to say such a thing?'

He looked at his unsmoked cigar and flung it out of the window with a smothered curse. 'I did it for you, you lying little bitch,' he said in a low bitter voice. 'I couldn't stand watching that woman insulting you. Hell, I don't know why I said it—it just came out.'

'Did you have to start being chivalrous at that particular moment?' Sophie moaned, half hysterical. 'It's so out of character, Mr Lefkas. Why couldn't you have picked someone else to play a knight in shining armour for?'

His eyes glittered as he stared at her. 'I wish to God I'd let her rant on,' he muttered. 'But you looked so damned helpless. I should just have slapped her round the face.'

'It would at least have been what I'd expect from you,' Sophie told him. 'And it wouldn't have left us with this problem.'

'There's no problem,' he said, starting the engine.

'How can you say that?'

'Easily,' he told her. 'In my experience the best way of handling a problem is to make it work for you.'

'You're insane,' Sophie said derisively. 'What do you mean, work for you?'

The car moved away, gathering speed as he turned towards her home. 'Get some profit out of it,' he said without looking at her.

Sophie tensed, watching his hard profile. 'What's that supposed to mean?'

His long hands moved capably on the wheel. He didn't look at her. 'I'm thinking it out,' he said. 'I'll let you know when I've seen the answer.'

There was a silence for a while, then Sophie pleaded softly, 'Let me tell Simon, explain to him . . .'

'No!' The word was snarled at her. Alex gave her a fixed, hard look. 'No. I want your word on that.'

Sophie lowered her voice, whispering, 'Can't you imagine how he must feel now?'

'Oh, yes,' said Alex almost with malice. 'I should say he's in hell, and even if you swore on your honour that there was nothing between you and me, he wouldn't believe you now. Not after seeing you in my arms, hearing

me say I was going to marry you. I'd say that right now
he hates the sound of your name.'

Sophie felt ice running over her skin. Yes, she thought.
He was right. Simon had looked at her with contempt
and hatred as he hustled Elaine away a moment after
Alex dropped his bombshell. Simon must believe her to
be a consummate liar. She had been so careful to assure
him that there was nothing between her and Alex.

'You'd only be wasting your time if you went to him
now and told him you were still faithful.' Alex gave her
a narrow-eyed, unpleasant smile. 'So I shouldn't bother.'

Another car blared past them, headlights blazing, and
Alex snapped an oath at the departing driver. He turned
into her road and pulled up, swinging to face her. 'Anyway, there's no future for you with him—you know that.
That wife of his isn't going to let him go. She has too
much to lose. She may hate his guts, but she loves his
house and money.'

'That's all she ever cared about,' Sophie said bitterly.

Alex drummed his fingers on the wheel. 'How long has
it gone on? Between you and him?'

Bending her head, Sophie muttered, 'Five years.'

'Five years? God, how old were you?'

'Eighteen,' she said on a long sigh.

'He ought to be bloody shot,' Alex snapped viciously.
'He's got to be all of forty.'

'He's thirty-eight.'

'And when he got hold of you he was thirty-three to
your eighteen? You were a sitting duck for him, I suppose. Bowled over by his looks and his money.'

'You can talk!' Sophie burst out furiously, hating him.
'How old is Patrice Lerrand? You've admitted to me that
you use your money to buy women. How dare you snipe
at Simon?'

'Five years,' Alex said slowly. 'And you expect me to

believe he's never had you?'

Her face washed a hot angry red. 'I don't ask you to believe anything. I don't care what you believe—it happens to be true. Simon isn't like you. He wouldn't press me to go to bed with him.'

'What is he, then? Some sort of freak? Carries on a love affair for five years and never tries to get you into bed? Do you think I'm stupid?'

'He loves me!'

'He wants you,' Alex said thickly. 'I watched the pair of you, remember. I didn't get the impression it was platonic. You were practically eating each other.'

'Oh, God!' Sophie moaned, dropping her face into her hands, sick at the thought of him watching them during those moments.

'Let's start again, shall we?' said Alex, bending towards her. 'I'll ask you once more and this time I want the truth. Have you been to bed with him, and how often?'

She didn't answer and he dragged her hands away from her face, forcing her chin up towards him. 'Have you? How many times? Where do you meet him?'

'Please,' she quivered, her lips shaking.

'Tell me.' His grey eyes held hers almost hypnotically, boring into her.

Sophie ran a dry tongue over her lips. 'I've scarcely been home over the past three years. I've seen him four times in that time, always with other people around. We haven't ever been alone.'

'Before that?' he asked tautly.

Her eyes tried to slide away and his fingers tightened, pushing her head back against the seat. He leaned over her, looking into her eyes. 'Before that?'

'We didn't make love,' Sophie said huskily. 'I would have, but Simon wouldn't.' Her mouth curved softly, tenderness in the movement. 'He said he felt guilty enough for having let me see how he felt.'

'Tell me everything from the beginning,' Alex said after a long moment. 'How did it start?'

Alex was imposing his will through the fixed stare of those grey eyes and Sophie felt herself weakening under that hypnotic power. 'Elaine and Simon had been married for five years, then Elaine began to have affairs with other men. Simon guessed, but Elaine was too careful. He could never be certain—she made sure of that. She somehow managed both to taunt him with them and to be too clever for him to prove anything. She was already drinking. She's gone away for treatment twice. Simon wanted a divorce before he fell in love with me, but when Elaine realised what he was going to do she started to be even more careful. She told him she was going to make it very hard for him. She didn't want a divorce. If he insisted, she said she would get custody of Lucy and take her away where Simon wouldn't see her.'

'Surely to God no judge would give that woman custody of a child!'

Sophie sighed deeply. 'The courts always lean over to the mother's side. In most cases they're right. Elaine would have stayed off the drink, put on an act to convince the court that she was a loving and devoted mother. Oh, Simon might have won—but he wouldn't take the risk of losing. He couldn't bear what Elaine would do to Lucy if she got her.'

'A leopard can't change its spots. Sooner or later, Elaine's real character would have come out and he would have got the child back.'

'But how long would it take? A year? Two? Can you imagine what a vicious woman could do to a child in two years?'

Alex stared at her. 'But surely even that woman wouldn't . . .'

'Elaine hates Lucy and she shows it—oh, not openly; in nasty little ways, smiles and words, things you can't put your finger on—Lucy is miserable every time she sees her mother. Simon makes sure she rarely does by having a nanny who guards Lucy night and day.' Sophie looked at him urgently. 'Elaine is capable of anything. She even once threatened to kidnap Lucy and smuggle her out of the country if Simon tried to divorce her. And she's determined enough to try. Simon was too scared of the consequences to risk it. He loves Lucy deeply.'

'More than he loves you,' said Alex in a curt cold voice.

'In a different way,' Sophie retorted.

'I saw how different,' Alex muttered. 'Very well. So how did he start this affair with you?'

'It just happened,' she whispered. How could she put into words that spring when she was eighteen and Simon turned his blue eyes on her, at first teasing, mocking her, laughter in his glance, only to have the laughter die and something far more dangerous take its place.

Alex was staring at her fixedly, as though obsessed with a need to know, to experience by proxy the abandoned passion he had seen in her as she kissed the other man. He caught at her shoulder, wrenching her towards him, and she cried out at the pain of his grip, her body arching, the movement seeming to excite him.

He bent his face so that his mouth almost touched hers and whispered, 'I want to know everything.'

'Don't,' begged Sophie in a trembling voice, staring back at him with troubled eyes, feeling the emotion inside him and not understanding.

His hand curved round her neck, feeling for the little blue vein which beat and betrayed her life. She shivered as his cool fingertips slowly caressed it. 'How did it start?'

Trembling, husky, she said: 'We were walking in the woods, talking, and I said something, I can't even remember what, but Simon looked at me, laughing, and then he stopped laughing. I don't even remember how, but then I was in his arms.' She stopped speaking, her throat hurting. She remembered the dousing of the light as passion became so urgent that the world seemed to recede to a great distance. Simon had never touched her before, never kissed her, and the pressure of unsatisfied desire had become intolerable. They almost went too far. Each caress had led to another, her tension and fever rising until her whole body was burning. If she dreamt of it, as she often did, she could smell the scent of crushed grass, hear the croon of wood pigeons in the trees around them and hear Simon gasping, groaning, crying out wildly as his body moved restlessly against hers.

Although she had stopped talking about it, Alex was watching her face, the coming and going of her colour, the feverish brilliance of her eyes, and he was reading all the things she wasn't telling him.

'It's going to stop,' he said harshly.

Sophie looked up at him, dazed. 'What?'

'It's over,' he said. 'From now on, you're going to forget him.'

She laughed hysterically. 'Do you really think I haven't tried? This past three years I've stayed away from my own home in order to try to forget him, and it hasn't worked.'

'It's easy to fool oneself,' Alex said almost gently. 'You've been telling yourself to forget him, perhaps, but you've been holding on to him in your head. You'll never be free until you let go.'

He was saying what she knew herself, but it was differ-

ent, hearing it from someone else, because for five years
she had been telling herself to forget Simon, and in all
those years she had been lying to herself. She didn't even
want to forget him. Her body, heart and mind were trapped in a memory so addictive that she would tear herself
apart if she tried to escape from it.

'I love him so much,' she said, looking at Alex pleadingly, and finding incredibly that it was a relief to be able
to say it aloud, that having someone know for the first
time was wonderful. She had hidden it for so long and
now it wasn't just her secret. Alex knew and she could
say it aloud. 'I love him,' she said again, smiling.

Alex didn't smile back. His face was masklike, rigid.
'Not any more,' he said coolly. 'You've wasted five years
of your life, but it's going to stop tonight. What point is
there in pouring yourself into the sand of a futile re-
lationship?'

'You can't turn off love!' Didn't he understand that?

'You're going to,' Alex said as casually as if it were
something simple, an everyday matter. He caught her
face between his hands, his palms cool against her flushed
skin and looked at her intently. 'Look at me.'

Sophie looked, frowning.

'Look at me, Sophie,' Alex said again, and she had a
weird sensation as if he had said it before more than
once, had been saying it for a long time. She stared, her
chin tilted as he held her face, the green eyes puzzled
and distressed, the cheeks stained with her tears, her pink
mouth trembling.

'You've let me get too close,' he said softly, as though,
oddly, he were taunting her. 'I imagine you never intended that to happen, but it has, and you're going to
look at me, and see me, Sophie.'

Her eyes widened in confusion. She stared as though
she had never seen him before and knew suddenly that

it was true. She had always kept that invisible barrier between them, between herself and every man she met, so that even Alex Lefkas had been somehow spectral to her, as though he were a visitant from another world and she couldn't feel or see him properly. Once or twice he had crashed his way through that barrier, but only briefly, but now he had somehow penetrated her force field, the personal barrier which isolated her from everyone she met. Alex was inside it now, standing in front of her, making her look at him.

The grey eyes were very hard and brilliant, glittering with force, all their power turned on her.

'I realised early on that I wasn't getting to you,' Alex said softly. 'I thought you were keeping me at arms' length in order to make me more interested, at first, and then I thought you had a plan to get me so desperate for you that I'd marry you. I couldn't believe you really weren't interested in me.'

Sophie smiled ruefully. 'I realised that. But I wasn't.'

'No,' he said in that soft careful tone, 'I know that now. Tell me one thing—why did you respond the way you did that night in London?'

Blushing hotly, she shook her head. 'I was drunk.'

'Don't lie,' Alex bit out, his hands biting into her face. 'Tell me the truth. Why?'

Trembling, she muttered, 'I'd been thinking of Simon.'

'Ah,' he said on a long breath. She felt the stiffening of his body and looked at him anxiously.

'So that's why I got a sudden response,' he said, and she felt an indefinable menace coming from him. 'Well, from now on you're going to forget he ever existed. You haven't really tried to forget him before. Now you will; I'll see that you do.'

Sophie looked at him in sudden, contemptuous suspicion. 'So that's what you meant about getting a profit

out of it! If you imagine you're going to take advantage
of this situation to get me into bed you're wrong!'

He gave her a long glance. 'You're forgetting something, aren't you? You owe me something.'

'I owe you what?'

'This,' he said, his head swooping. The brutal, possessive demand of his mouth opened her lips as she
tried to protest. Alex gave a thick groan of satisfaction, taking full advantage of her parted, moaning
mouth.

'No,' she groaned, struggling.

The kiss deepened hotly. Alex slid his arms under her
body, lifting her towards him. His mouth moved harshly, bruising her lips. Suddenly she began to hear the
muffled thud of his heart. He was breathing thickly,
rapidly, his body urgently touching hers. His excitement
communicated itself to her like a spark leaping through
brushfire. Her body began to tremble. She fought
against the sensual impact of what he was doing, feeling
the long hands travelling up and down her back,
moulding her body closer to him. 'No,' she moaned
again, and he kissed her even more demandingly, lying
on her now, one thigh thrust between hers, holding her
trapped. Her mind submerged. With a wild hoarse cry
she yielded, and Alex's heartbeat quickened as he felt
her weaken and give herself to his passion.

Moments later he sat up, and Sophie lay with closed
eyes and a deeply flushed face, breathing roughly,
trembling.

Alex had drunk from her softly yielding mouth like a
man who has thirsted too long and refuses to stop. He
had taken all he wanted, draining her, and Sophie felt
too dazed to move, shaken by the revelation of what
passion could do to her body. Alex could have pushed
her surrender to the limit, but he had stopped voluntari-

ly. All the same, her body bore the marks of his passion. Her dress had been half removed, the glimmer of her skin visible now in the shadowed car.

Alex leant over her, pulling up her dress, zipping it, tidying her hair briskly. 'You'd better go in,' he said. 'God knows what your parents think is going on out here.' He laughed drily. 'Exactly what has been going on, I suppose. Their worst fears confirmed.'

Sophie had to force her heavy lids open to look at him. Her green eyes were drowsy, dilated, her pink mouth swollen by the unsated demand he had made on it. She looked at him in confused incredulity, shaking from head to foot. The heat inside her body had not subsided when Alex moved away and she was utterly shaken by what he had aroused in her.

Alex eyed her sardonically. 'You look drunk.'

'I feel it,' she whispered through her bruised lips.

'If your family hear about the engagement, you're not to deny it,' he told her coolly.

'But—' she began, and he cut her off tersely.

'You're to say it's true.'

'Alex—' she began, and again he interrupted.

'I mean it.'

'We can't pretend! You haven't thought what that would mean! Your mother—your family. Oh, God, the newspapers! We have to stop it now before it goes any further.'

'It's going all the way,' said Alex, and she looked at him in total bewilderment.

'I'm marrying you,' he said shortly, watching her.

She felt a slow icy shiver run down her body. 'That isn't funny!'

'It wasn't meant to be.'

She swallowed and tried to speak lightly, mocking

him. 'You've forgotten about your plans, the girls your
family have picked out for you! You can't marry someone like me—you said so yourself.'

'None of that matters any more,' Alex told her with a
hard, dry smile.

She couldn't believe he was serious, staring at him
fixedly. 'I don't understand.'

'You will,' said Alex almost with menace, his grey eyes
piercing her face.

He must have drunk too much at the party, Sophie
thought, keeping her eyes on the strong dark face. He
didn't know what he was saying. He couldn't be serious.

Quite gently, she laid her hand on his arm and said:
'Alex, I do appreciate what you did for me when you
shut Elaine up, and I'm grateful. It was one of the worst
moments of my life and I don't want you to think I'm
ungrateful.'

His lips drew back in a snarl of cold laughter. 'I should
wait until we're married before you tell me how grateful
you are.'

Sophie's hand moved away from him, she stared at
him, frowning, confused and uneasy.

'I can't marry you,' she burst out.

'You will,' Alex said very, very softly, but there was
no teasing intimacy in his voice now, only a silky threat
his eyes underlined.

'You made a fool of me,' he said in that soft voice. 'I
told you. Nobody does that to me. I've wanted you for
months and now I'm going to have you.' He smiled
cruelly at her, his mouth sharp and predatory. 'And the
fact that you're going to hate every minute of it will make
it all the more interesting.'

'My God, you're crazy!' Sophie burst out, horrified.

'Crazy or not, that's the way it's going to be.'

She sat and stared at him, realising suddenly that under

the mask of that hard face was a terrible anger. Alex
was burning with rage. She hadn't seen it until now, she
had been too obsessed with her own feelings to notice
his, but now she looked into the cruel grey eyes and she
was afraid. She had let him get too close, he had said.
But who had she let get too close? What sort of man was
he? He talked with icy determination of marrying her,
knowing she didn't want him, forcing her to take him. It
was a punishment for what had happened tonight, she
thought. Alex meant to make her suffer for loving Simon,
as though in some odd way he felt she had betrayed him
by not loving him.

'Did you think I was in love with you?' she whispered.

Alex stared at her with icy hostility. 'Yes,' he said.

'Oh.' Sophie shivered. 'But why?'

'I thought you loved me because you wouldn't let me
make love to you,' Alex said, and Sophie shook her head
as though her brain were full of buzzing insects.

'You're crazy,' she said again.

'When you started to cry that morning in London, after
having been so passionate in my arms the night before,
I was fool enough to begin to think you really cared. It
was the only thing that made sense. Why do you think
I came down here after you? I was going to start again
with you, find out if the way I felt was serious. I thought
I might even fall in love with you. The first time in my
life I ever felt I might actually believe love could be possible for me, and then I find out you'd lied and cheated
me, like all the others. Women are born liars. I must have
been nuts to let you fool me into thinking you might be
different. But knowing what a damned little bitch you are
doesn't stop me wanting your body, and you're going to
pay for having pulled the wool over my eyes. I told you,
nobody makes a fool of me and gets away with it.'

'I didn't make a fool of you!'

'You did,' he said through his teeth.

'I didn't tell you about Simon because it was nothing to do with you. For heaven's sake, that sort of thing isn't something you write down in a letter applying for a job! It was my business, nobody else's. And anyway, I've never wanted you to be interested in me—I've tried to make that clear to you. I didn't want to marry you or go to bed with you or have you anywhere near me!'

Saying that was a mistake, because she felt the rage leaping up in his grey eyes, his teeth meeting like the snap of a steel trap.

'Protest all you like,' Alex said hoarsely. 'You're marrying me—if I have to handcuff you to get you to the church.'

CHAPTER EIGHT

SOPHIE came downstairs next morning to realise that her family had heard. It was obvious from the way they were talking urgently, in low, excited voices before she entered the kitchen, only to stop dead as the door opened. Their heads swung round and for a few seconds she saw the dazed, flushed disbelief in their faces, then they all smiled, moved, so that the tableau became once more a moving picture.

They didn't refer to Alex; they didn't ask any questions. Sophie got the feeling that they had discussed how they were to approach the matter and had decided on this pretence of knowing nothing, waiting for her to tell them.

It was a Saturday morning. Sophie had slept late after her over-exhausting experiences the night before—quite drained by the emotional shocks which had been aimed at her one after the other. She felt numb and cold and deeply anxious this morning, and it was quite an achievement for her to summon up a smile for her family. She was grateful for their discretion and had absolutely no intention of saying anything to them. Last night she had just fallen into bed and into sleep almost in the same motion. Her night had been heavy, her dreams chilling; nightmares of flight and pursuit, a sensation of trapped helplessness.

This morning she was going to have to see Alex, talk to him, get him to understand the folly of what he had suggested last night. Sophie was sure he would have changed his mind this morning. Last night he had been slightly the worse for drink—not drunk, admittedly, but under the influence of drink, all the same. He had also been in a flaming temper. This morning he would be seeing things quite differently; Sophie was sure he would be ready to sort out this muddle now.

It was such a wild, absurd suggestion. Only a few days ago he had said to her that it was out of the question for him to marry a girl like her—and she had agreed with him. She hadn't wanted to marry him, of course, but from a purely rational point of view Alex Lefkas was right. A man in his position had to marry someone suitable—someone of his own class and wealth, someone who would fit into his world.

Sophie wasn't quite sure she understood what had prompted him to make that astounding announcement last night—mistaken chivalry, a sense of outrage at Elaine's spite, a crazy impulse which he must now be deeply regretting.

What he had said to her later, in the car, had been even more puzzling. She had been taken aback to find out that Alex honestly had imagined that she was in love with him, but his savage insistence that he was going to marry her to punish her for having deceived him was obviously just a temporary fit of anger.

He would have changed his mind this morning. So Sophie smiled at her family, ate a light breakfast and waited nervously for the phone to ring and Alex to tell her that he would unravel the tangled threads of their situation.

The phone did start ringing, but it wasn't Alex. Sophie answered it and was taken by surprise to be told it was the local paper. Before she could react, the young man at the other end was asking her eager, over-polite questions to which she could only mumble, 'No comment.' She hurriedly said she had to go and hung up, biting her lip. The phone rang again. Sophie looked at it as if it were a snake which was about to bite her.

'Shall I answer it?'

Patsy took her by surprise, too, her face quietly under-standing and very adult.

Sophie nodded. 'Don't tell them anything,' she added huskily.

Patsy gave her a dry little smile. 'How could I tell them something I don't know?'

Flushing, Sophie moved away and heard her sister smoothly telling whoever was on the phone that nobody had anything to say. Patsy hung up and the door bell rang.

'Oh, no!' Sophie whispered.

'I'll go,' Patsy told her. 'Keep out of sight.'

Sophie went into the kitchen and rushed past her silent, watchful parents into the garden. The sun was already warming the air. A heavy drone of bees moved the roses. She looked up involuntarily towards Dancing Court and her body clenched against the pain invading it.

Oh, God, she thought, Simon. My poor Simon. Last night Alex had said maliciously that he would hate her now, and Sophie guessed he was right. Simon thought she was a liar, a cheat. It was unbearable to know how he must despise her.

Why didn't Alex ring? Was he still asleep? She knew he usually got up very early; his habits were already well known to her. Alex worked hard, even at the villa. He rose as early as Sophie did and he was at work im-mediately after breakfast. He did a lot of his work on the phone, talking to the various parts of the Lefkas empire, consulting with his executives around the world, giving orders and getting advice. Although he was relaxing when he was at the Crete villa, he always arrived loaded down with paperwork which he got through somehow.

But last night she had the feeling he would have gone

to sleep very late indeed. She didn't even know where he was—he hadn't told her. Maybe he had driven back to London.

She walked to and fro shivering, despite the warmth of the sun. She didn't know if she could face the questions, the stares, the inquisitive probing of neighbours, relatives, the press. She needed Alex's presence to cope with all that. She just did not know what to do. Last night she had been coerced into promising him not to deny their engagement. She wouldn't break her word. But he must get here soon, or ring her and give her permission to tell the truth.

Looking up, she found him standing there watching her and ran towards him, almost sick with relief. 'Alex —thank God! Alex, it's started. She's been talking. You've got to stop it!'

He took her shoulders in his hands and bent his head to kiss her and Sophie put her hands to his chest to push him away. The hands tightened, dug into her. His mouth covered hers firmly, possessively.

When he drew away he looked at her in cool appraisal. 'Get it through your head. You are marrying me.'

She had relied so heavily on a belief that this morning he would see reason that she couldn't speak, only stare dumbly at him, shaking her head.

He watched her, his smile derisive.

'You can't mean it,' she whispered at last. 'Alex, for God's sake!'

'I mean it,' he assured her. 'Did you think I was playing games? I was deadly serious.'

White-lipped, Sophie muttered, 'You can't make me marry you.'

'I can and will,' Alex promised with mockery. 'You have a simple choice, Sophie. Either you come quietly or you make me use force. If you accept that it's going to happen you'll be wise. If you force me to coerce you, I may not use pretty methods.'

Her green eyes lifted incredulously, searchingly to his face. He smiled at her as though he was saying something amusing, something teasing.

'I'll stop at nothing to get my own way—haven't you learnt that?' He put a hand against her cheek and stroked the curve of it with his fingertips. From the house it must have looked as though they were having a loving, intimate conversation. Sophie's face was hidden. Alex was facing the house and smiling all the time, smiling down at her, caressing her as he spoke. The charm and teasing smiles were all a surface mask. Under that the grey eyes were locked in ice.

He meant it.

'My mother's here,' he said, and watched the flare of hope in her eyes with comprehending sarcasm. 'But if you say one word to her to make her suspicious, you'll be sorry.'

Sophie had moved on instinct, about to run to Madame, to ask her for help. She looked up at Alex and he said softly: 'Be warned now, Sophie. I want my mother to believe we're in love. She already thought so; it wasn't hard to convince her. But if she sees you looking like death, she'll start to wonder. When you go in there, you'll smile if it kills you.'

'Why are you doing this to me?' Sophie asked shakily.

His eyes leapt with a sudden savagery. 'I told you last night.'

He moved restlessly and the morning sunlight suddenly picked out for her a weariness in his face, tension in the hard bones. Alex might be talking coolly, but under that there was a more human reaction to what was happening.

Without thinking, she lifted a hand to run along his cheek, feeling the taut features with her fingertips. 'It's madness,' she whispered. 'Alex, please, be reasonable!'

'Put your arms round my neck and kiss me,' he said instead of answering her. 'My mother is at the window.'

Sophie's hand quivered against his face. 'Don't,' she muttered.

'Kiss me,' said Alex through his tight lips.

His eyes held her own. Slowly she put her arms round his neck and leant forward. Alex's arms closed round her, pulling her closer. Their lips clung briefly, then he lifted his head, smiling with his mouth and never with his eyes.

'Now we'll go in,' he said softly. 'And you will convince my mother you are rapturously happy. Not one sign of anything else, Sophie, or you'll regret it.'

She swallowed, glancing past him towards Dancing Court. The sycamore leaves were turning and rustling in a windy dance, making black patterns on the turf. Sheep quietly moved in the park and there were little white clouds moving like sheep in the blue sky. Alex watched the movement of her eyes and his hard eyes narrowed.

'I told you—forget him. He never existed. Face it, you can never have him, and you can't go on living an empty life.'

Would life be any the less empty for marrying another man? she thought with pain.

'Smile,' Alex said insistently. 'You can act, Sophie. I watched you act like hell last night, all the time the two of you were together, smiling at each other like old acquaintances when all the time you were secret lovers. So you can act like that now.'

He put his arm around her waist and led her towards the house. Sophie pulled herself together, somehow managed to drag a smile on to her face as Madame held out her arms to her.

'Sophie, child—I knew! I knew almost from the start.'

Sophie was in her arms, kissed firmly, smiled at with love. 'I'm so happy,' Madame told her, her dark eyes dancing with pleasure. 'I'd begun to think my wicked Alex would never know what it was to fall in love until I saw the way he was looking at you.'

'You're just self-satisfied because it was you who found her,' Alex said lightly. 'I'll never hear the end of it, I suppose—the crowing and gloating over my downfall! You were plotting against me, Mama. Come on, confess it!'

'I'm not ashamed of it,' Madame nodded, smiling at him, still holding Sophie in one arm. 'I was delighted when I realised you'd met your Waterloo.'

Sophie glanced nervously at her own family. Alex glanced at them, too, smiling carefully. 'I've explained that I asked you not to break the news until Mama and I got here, darling. I think your parents were a little hurt that you hadn't told them.'

'I'm sorry.' Sophie whispered, looking at her mother and then her father. 'But Alex wanted it this way.'

'Oh, I knew all the offhand talk about not knowing him very well was just a smokescreen,' Patsy told her brightly. 'Especially last night. We're not dumb, you know.'

'Far from it,' said Alex, smiling teasingly at her, and Patsy grew pink and grinned back at him with very big eyes. Alex using his charm like mad, Sophie thought cynically. She could tell that her family were shattered by the news, but her mother was so excited she was almost frenetic, her eyes feverishly bright, moving restlessly in her chair, looking from Alex to Sophie ecstatically.

'I won't ask you your prospects,' her father said, chuckling at his own humour.

'I don't think you need fear that Sophie will ever

starve,' Alex agreed, sliding an arm around her and detaching her from his mother. He looked down at her. 'I know how to look after my own.'

Sophie quelled a faint shiver at the words.

'Now,' said Madame, 'What are we going to do about the wedding? I'm afraid that our family are going to want it to take place in our own country. I can understand that you would rather have it here, of course, but perhaps we could come to some compromise—a dual ceremony?'

Sophie's teeth sank into her lower lip. She felt sick at this talk of a wedding. Alex was watching her and he interrupted his mother quietly: 'We'll be married in Crete,' he said. 'Sophie wants that. Of course, any members of her family who wish to attend will be flown out to be there, but the wedding will be held in our own local church in Crete.'

Sophie felt her mother's disappointment, the sigh she gave, but her father said at once: 'We only want Sophie to be happy.' He grinned at Alex frankly. 'I've no doubt it would be better if you were married on your own ground. Your family would expect it.'

Sophie realised that her father had been somewhat appalled at the expense of a wedding which was bound to attract so many wealthy guests—his modest income wouldn't have stretched far enough to pay for the sort of reception the Lefkas family would expect. Her mother, of course, starry-eyed over the whole thing, hadn't even considered the cost. She would have been happy to mortgage her whole future to give Sophie a wonderful wedding.

Patsy was bubbling over with chatter about it all. Madame sat-listening to her, smiling with amusement, but Sophie couldn't wait to get away. She was finding it all too much of a strain to keep this fixed smile on her face. When Alex and Madame had gone, she realised, she was going to be asked a lot of searching questions. Her family were dying to ask her things they couldn't quite dare to ask under Alex's eyes. She hated the thought of lying to them.

She might have known Alex would have thought of all that. 'I'm afraid we're going to have to take Sophie with us,' he told her family lightly. 'If she stayed here, the press would be all over the house like wasps around a honey jar.' He paused, smiling crookedly. 'And I want her with me,' he added, deliberately rueful.

Everyone laughed. 'Well, that's honest,' her father said, puffing at his pipe, looking so comfortingly himself that Sophie longed to run and beg him to help her, but knew she couldn't do it.

'I'll go and pack,' she said.

She had to face a few moments alone with her mother, of course. Mrs Bryant hugged her, eyes sparkling. 'Of course, we guessed! When he arrived like that out of the blue— I knew it meant something of the sort, and he was so charming to us when he picked you up. I could tell he was making a special effort to get to know us. You've been very secretive, Sophie. You might have dropped a few hints.'

Sophie bent her face over the case she was packing. 'I didn't want to say anything until I was sure,' she said.

'I can understand that. It's like a fairy story. Oh, I'm so excited, Sophie! How can you be so calm about it all? His mother's nice, very nice. You said she was a darling, but you were very devious about him. You told us he was a Don Juan! I quite thought you meant it at the time. And all the time you were in love with him! You've always been a very quiet girl. Still waters run deep.'

Elaine had said that, Sophie thought. She hadn't liked it then and she didn't like it now.

'Did he mean it about the family? Will he fly us out? Anyone who's left out of the invitations is going to be very offended, that's the trouble. We'll have to put our heads together, darling, and draw up a list. When are you planning to have it? I suppose it will take a time for the arrangements to be made. It will be such a big wedding, he must know so many people he'll want to invite.'

Please, please, Sophie thought despairingly, stop talking about it! She went on packing, not answering, and her mother didn't wait for answers, too excited to do anything but spill out eager happy words, her eyes so bright she looked half drunk.

There was a tap at the door and Alex came into the room. He searched Sophie's eyes. 'Ready, darling?' Coming forward, he closed her case and firmly locked it. 'I'm afraid there are some press outside. They've been ringing at the door. Your sister is going hoarse telling them to go away.'

Her mother went to the window and peered out. 'Good heavens, there's a crowd outside!'

'I'm afraid the presence of the reporters and cameramen has caused a little local excitement,' Alex said drily. He was looking down at Sophie behind her mother's back, his brows drawn. 'Don't say a word to them,' he ordered softly. 'Just leave it all to me.'

She nodded. He put an arm round her and Sophie felt so tired she leaned on him with a long sigh and felt his hand tighten on her. He put his lips against her hair and she closed her eyes, willing all this to be a dream from which she would wake at any moment.

She opened her eyes and it was all still there, and her mother was looking at her and Alex with smiling eyes, seeing in their entwined bodies and Alex's gentle caress an indication of love.

'Come on,' said Alex, moving with her to the door.

'We have to face them. If we wait much longer, the crowd will get bigger.'

They had to fight their way through the press of curious people to the limousine. The chauffeur irritably pushed people back, held Madame's arm to help her into the car. Alex had Sophie firmly in his arm and merely shook his head to all the shouted questions. Sophie was pale and shivering as the car door finally shut. The limousine moved away and cameras flashed outside the windows. Faces peered and hands waved. As though they were royalty, she thought bitterly.

'Thank heavens that's over,' sighed Madame. 'What are you going to do, Alex?'

'London first,' he said. 'Then you and Sophie go back to Crete. I'll have the wedding details worked out when I've had a look at my schedule for the year. You and Sophie can make guest lists. I suggest you limit them to immediate family and really close friends.'

Sophie sat back in the car with his thigh against her own and heard him and his mother talking across her. It wasn't real, she thought. It wasn't happening. It was all a wild surrealist dream and she would wake up some day to discover she had imagined the whole thing.

The week that followed was hectic. She and Madame remained in London, but Sophie found herself now on permanent display. Members of the Lefkas family, friends of Madame, arrived to meet her and stare in searching and slightly incredulous curiosity at her. She was not the sort of wife they had all imagined Alex Lefkas would finally choose. They knew nothing about her or her family. Alex, she saw, was thought to have gone mad. Infatuation, she heard one slightly deaf aunt whisper to another, quite unaware that Sophie could hear them. 'A lovely girl, but really! Is Alex out of his mind?'

Yes, Sophie thought, he is totally out of his mind. With

every passing day she was more sure of that. She knew from having lived with Madame all these months that the world in which Alex moved was not her world. She wasn't fitted for it in any way.

She began to believe, to hope, that Alex would realise what folly he was committing, and break their engagement. She had seen almost nothing of him since they got back to London. He almost seemed to be avoiding her and she began to think that that was precisely what he was doing—perhaps he was searching for some honourable way out of the dilemma he had created for himself.

The night before she and Madame flew back to Crete, Madame said teasingly to Alex at dinner: 'Now, you've hardly seen Sophie since we got here—tonight I'm going to play Cupid and leave the two of you alone. I shall get an early night. I hate these long flights, as you know. I need to be well prepared for them!'

Sophie's throat closed in alarm as Madame left them. She was sitting beside Alex on the couch drinking coffee and he caught the quick, nervous look she gave him. His grey eyes flashed.

'Stop looking at me as if I were a dangerous lunatic!'

Sophie glanced down at her coffee cup. 'There's still time to tell them we've changed our minds,' she muttered.

'But we haven't.' His voice was clear and cool.

'Alex!'

'Don't Alex me,' he said impatiently. 'Stop wriggling around looking for some escape hatch. We're getting married and that's that.'

'You're just being pig-headed!' Sophie flared, giving him a look from angry green eyes.

He moved closer and took her cup. 'I think you need something stronger than that,' he said drily, sardonic eyes noting her startled glance. Rising, he strolled over to the decanters and poured them both some whisky, adding soda to her glass before moving back towards her with them both.

She looked at the glass doubtfully and he pressed it into her hand, observing her with mocking amusement. 'Drink it and relax,' he ordered.

Sophie raised her eyes to the hard, sardonic face with a deep hostility. 'You're enjoying this!'

'That's right,' he said softly. 'And I shall enjoy it more and more. Drink your whisky.'

She looked down at the amber liquid and knew he was right—she needed some stimulus to get her through these last tense moments with him.

Although she wasn't looking at him, she was very aware of the intent stare of those grey eyes, and she was beginning to be frightened of him.

Alex had only wanted to take her to bed at first: he had admitted that. It was her own fault that he had begun to think of her in a different way. Her passionate response the night he made love to her here, in this room, had made him imagine that although she was refusing to let him seduce or buy her, she was secretly in love with him. For some reason Alex had been touched by that. When she burst into tears and ran away from him the morning she left London, she had pricked his conscience and he had followed her because his feelings had taken a sudden change. Alex had begun to think he might really be falling in love with her. She could understand the surprise he must have felt. He was a man who had always regarded women with acquisitive indulgent contempt. There had been so many of then in his life; Sophie knew that. Alex had never expected to fall in love. He hadn't even believed in love.

Then he had seen her wild response to another man and known that he had been wrong about her feelings towards himself. He was angry. He was burning with rage because he felt she had made a fool of him. He wouldn't accept that he had made a fool of himself; he blamed her for everything.

Sophie saw that if she did marry him, he would make her pay for it all. He wanted to see her suffer. He was brushing aside her feelings for Simon, but he wasn't forgetting them, although he was insisting that she should. For the moment, Alex was totally absorbed in getting her. It was when he had got her that all the rage would finally emerge from under that deceptively charming face.

He wasn't touching her, but she felt the desire to hurt which raged in him. The night he had made forcible love to her in his car outside her home, she had glimpsed some of what was seething beneath his mask. That had been the tip of the iceberg. Since then, he had hidden the cruel necessity which was driving him, but Sophie felt it, all the same, and shivered with fear.

She should have made it completely clear to him in the beginning that she didn't find him attractive. She had thought she was doing so, but obviously she hadn't tried hard enough.

Or had that been exactly what fed his feelings for her? Was Alex so competitive that he took rejection merely as a challenge? She knew that the strong drive which made him a brilliant executive must fuel his other reactions too. Had he been so determined purely because he knew very well that he wasn't getting anywhere? Maybe if she had been a push-over for him in the beginning he would have walked away, bored with an easy conquest.

Whatever the causes of his present mood, he frightened her. There was so much dark intent behind that face of his—Sophie wasn't sure exactly what he was hiding, but she did not like it, whatever it was.

Suddenly he moved, disturbing her agitated thoughts, taking her empty glass from her and putting it down on

the table. Sophie looked at him anxiously as he turned
back towards her.

Of course, she had been anticipating such a move, but
now that he was making it, she could not help trembling,
muttering drily, 'Please, don't, Alex.'

'Don't?' His face was cruel, his smile a savage twist of
his lips. 'Why do you think I'm doing all this? I'm pay-
ing a very high price for you, Sophie. I intend to get total
satisfaction for it.'

She shook her head, paling. 'Must you be so brutal?'

'I haven't even started yet,' he promised softly, staring
at her mouth. His lids moved down over the grey eyes
until he looked almost sleepy, a cynical brooding expression in his face. 'My God, I want you,' he muttered abruptly before his mouth came down hungrily, parting her
trembling lips and almost suffocating her with the deep,
insistent demand he made on her. Sophie struggled to
keep herself free of the drugging movements of that kiss,
but a spark from Alex's leaping fire spread to her own
body. As she moaned helplessly, his hands began to
caress her body and she felt a curious weakness invading
her, as if her bones were melting in her feverish trembling
flesh.

It had happened before. The night he made love to her
in his car she had finally given in to the stark compulsion
of his desire, and now it happened again.

She tried to halt the increasing wildness of her response,
putting her hands against his chest and pushing him
away. 'No!' she moaned, looking at him with terror.

'You want it,' he said hoarsely. 'You need it. Do you
think your body doesn't tell me that?'

She shook her head violently, half sobbing, her face
white, and Alex held her, the hard pressure of his body
forcing her back against the couch. 'Yes,' he said thickly.
'You've been pushing it all down out of sight for five

bloody years, but it's there and I'm going to have it.
You're going to give me all the passion you've never
been able to give him. I want it all.' He took her face in
his hands, staring into her dazed green eyes, his face
cruel. 'Everything inside you,' he told her with a savagery
which appalled her.

She was so terrified she managed to break away from
him, only to have him fling her back on the couch, his
body imposed brutally on her, holding her down beneath
him, the powerful thighs controlling her as she struggled
to get away.

Her shaking made Alex so angry that his face tightened even more, his eyes icy. 'You little bitch,' he muttered in that hoarse, bitter voice. 'I'm going to have you
and if you fight, I'll hurt you, I promise that.'

She had known that this was under the calm face he
had shown over the last week. Her instincts had warned
her. But she hadn't guessed it was so deep and savage a
feeling, and it shocked her into lying shivering in his
hands while he opened her evening blouse with rapid,
angry fingers and pushed her bra strap down over one
shoulder. The glitter of his eyes as he cupped her breast
made Sophie draw a long, protesting breath. He looked
up at her, his fingers fondling her white smooth skin,
shaping and possessing it, then his eyes darkened, as
though he was angered even further by her mute, shaking
resistance.

The black head swooped. His mouth made ruthless
contact with hers, bruised, crushed, demanded. Sophie
could never remember afterwards at what point she
fainted. One moment she was tremblingly engulfed by
that hard, forceful mouth, the heated movements of his
hands over her body; the next she was flutteringly opening her lids as though they were weighted with lead, so
cold that she shivered and her teeth chattered.

Alex was kneeling beside the couch, a glass of water in his hand. He was white, too, but the grey eyes were a remorseless obsidian.

Her physical escape from him had angered him more than ever. He observed her return to consciousness coldly. Lifting her head from the pillows he had placed beneath it, he made her sip the water. When she had drunk enough he lowered her head and turned to put down the glass.

Dishevelled, distraught, she watched him as he looked back at her.

'You'd better go to bed,' he said in flat controlled tones. He helped her up, supporting her when her weak legs almost collapsed under her, and she leaned on him helplessly, her head against his chest, hearing the rapid thud of his heart under her ear. Alex gave a muttered exclamation, then picked her up in his arms like a child, her head flung back over one strong arm. He carried her down the corridor to her room, thrusting open her door with one foot. When he lowered her to the bed she lay there watching him in the darkness like a trapped animal, a rabbit waiting for the remorseless blow from the poacher's hand.

'No,' he said as he understood why she was staring at him with that fixed, helpless rigidity, 'I'm not going to take you tonight. I'll wait. But don't imagine for one second that you're ever getting away from me, Sophie. I meant what I said. You'll only make me angrier if you try to escape me now.'

She didn't answer, shuddering.

After a moment he said in that cool, controlled voice: 'Do you want me to help you undress?'

'No,' she whispered thinly.

He smiled in sardonic appreciation. 'I had a feeling

you might not.' He moved to the door and paused, looking back at her. 'Goodnight, Sophie.'

The door shut and she lay there, feeling as though it was not only a physical darkness which was surrounding her. Despite her suspicions about Alex's anger she had had no real idea of the depth of his rage. Tonight it had come leaping out of him, dragging her down into a hellish compulsion which had left her drained and exhausted. And he was right—it hadn't even started yet. They weren't married. When they were, Sophie knew she was going to start to learn just how cruel Alex could be—that dark Greek face held disturbing, primitive echoes of an ancient barbarism which more civilised times had suppressed but which could still be glimpsed in the faded frescoes and icons of the past. Deep ocean tides of ancestry, stored, spiralled and unseen, in the genetic cells but freed by some triggering impulse, were alive in him now.

Her rejection of him had unwittingly touched off this explosion, awoken the hereditary savage sleeping inside his twentieth-century mind. All in Sophie herself that was a product of her time and education, her liberated common sense, rose up in protest at what she had seen in Alex tonight. Her brain invoked the sanity of fact against the threat she had sensed in him. He could not force her to marry him. She was free, her own possession, nobody could make her do anything. She lay trembling in that darkness and felt the pressure of the elements man had so long suppressed mocking her.

Alex had not been joking. She faced that, biting her lip. He wasn't going to let her get away from him.

CHAPTER NINE

THREE months later Sophie stood on the powdered coral sand of a Caribbean beach, watching the brilliant blue water cream slowly over her feet and ebb away again. The sky echoed the unbelievable colour of the water, cloudless, burning in the afternoon heat. At her back lay the serrated frondlike green of massed palm trees, stirring gently in the faint sea breeze, pierced by sunlight here and there, with the white arches and walls of the villa in which she and Alex were to spend their honeymoon shimmering in the light.

They had arrived very late last night. Sophie had been so tired she had barely been able to undress. Alex had gone to his own room without a word as soon as they arrived. She had even been too tired to be grateful for that.

The last months had been a peculiar, trancelike period when she moved like a zombie towards her marriage without ever really believing it would happen or without ever making any real attempt to stop it. She worked with Madame on the arrangements without thinking about what they meant to herself. Sometimes, unwrapping the hundreds of gifts which had poured into the villa, she had looked dumbly around her with a doped dullness, her pale face struggling to break free of the trap closing in on her.

She had seen almost nothing of Alex in those months, yet he never left her thoughts. He was burning himself into her mind, like redhot metal smouldering its way through fragile gauze. Her sleep was haunted by him.

149

Watching Madame in the sunlit autumnal garden she felt a need for flight warring with a residual primitive fear of pursuit, and so she went on; opening presents, answering letters, having fittings for her wedding gown, going through the motions of a bride without being more than half aware of what she was doing.

In that half-life she found images and memories of Simon hard to recapture. She had no emotion inside her but fear.

She even managed to open a present from Elaine and Simon without breaking into tears, reading the spiteful little note from Elaine which came with it without a flicker.

'Congratulations, Sophie darling. So clever of you. I don't have to tell you Simon sends his love.'

Holding the card between restless, twisting fingers, Sophie slowly tore it across and dropped it into the large cardboard box holding wrapping paper and string to be burnt by Hector later.

Alex arrived at the villa two days before the wedding, and if his quick, cool eyes saw through her controlled mask, he said nothing and did nothing to increase her fear.

Madame's happiness was the only genuine feeling of joy in the rooms of the villa before the wedding guests began to arrive. Sophie found it hardest to face Madame's warm dark eyes with a smile. She was smiling all the time, of course, but only she knew how hard it was to make the facial movements look genuine.

Alex had rented several other villas to take those guests from other parts of the world who would need accommodation, but Sophie's parents and Patsy stayed in the Lefkas villa itself, and she acted more and more as the actual wedding day arrived.

Looking back on it now, she could barely remember

any individual moments of it, except her shiver of submission when Alex and she exchanged rings and she felt
his long fingers touch her own.

That moment had been the instant when the smouldering iron reached her centre and she trembled from head
to foot as Alex shot her a hard, insistent look.

She hadn't noticed anyone at the reception. People
had stood and talked to her and she had spoken to them,
she supposed. Faces had loomed and vanished in the
room. She had been kissed over and over again, but only
once by Alex, and then it had been a brief courteous touch
of his mouth which did not present any demand.

Elaine and Simon had been invited, automatically, by
her mother, but although she imagined they had been
present, Sophie couldn't even remember seeing them. The
thought that Simon had been in the same room without
her noticing him made her understand how far Alex had
isolated her from the whole world. He had marked her,
singled her out, driven her from the human herd, and she
had no idea how to find her way back. The symbolic en-
closure of his ring over her finger had completed her total
possession by him.

She was still wandering in the limbo of alienation now,
silent and pale, having scarcely seen him today. He had
been working when Sophie got up. The lighthearted servants who ran the villa served her a breakfast of coffee
and fruit, and told her, grinning, that 'Mr Alex' was talking on the phone to New York.

What they thought of a man who worked even on his
honeymoon, Sophie did not care. She had been too grateful to be left alone. She had seen him at lunch, been
treated with a display of charming courtesy which seemed
to go down well with the servants anyway, and then left
to her own devices while Alex went back to the phone.

'There's been some trouble in Venezuela,' he told her.

'We're having difficulties finding out what has gone wrong. I shouldn't be long now.'

The villa lay in a smooth-lawned expanse of trees and flowers which covered twenty acres and which included a private beach made idyllic by a fringe of palm trees. There was no way to the beach except either through the villa grounds or over steep rocky cliffs dense with low scrub. The servants had smilingly assured Sophie that she would not be disturbed by anyone down there.

The sand had a pale pinkish colour, the tiny powdered grains of coral clinging like sugar to her feet as she walked down to the water. Her bikini, like the rest of her clothes, was new; Madame had insisted on a full trousseau which they had bought in Athens and Paris. Sophie could remember sitting on a tiny gilt chair looking without interest at the models walking past her, smiling when Madame seemed pleased, shrugging when Madame looked doubtful. Sophie hadn't chosen any of the clothes herself, she had merely acquiesced in Madame's choice.

Hearing the sound of other feet padding over the beach, she turned and saw Alex walking towards her in brief black swimming trunks. His long lean body moved with muscled ease in the sunlight.

'Have you sorted out the problem?' Sophie looked away as she spoke because the impact of his body was sending shivers running through her.

'Satisfactorily,' he agreed with a dry and sardonic note she did not miss. 'Are you coming in or are you going to stand there and look ravishing for me while I swim?'

Without answering she waded forward into the blue water until it would support her body, diving forward gracefully and striking out towards the ocean.

'Watch the coral reefs!' Alex shouted just behind her.

'Don't go too close. Some coral is just below the water level.'

'Yes,' she said, beginning to float on her back, her arms spread out to keep her buoyant, staring up at the blue arch of the sky. A few seabirds skimmed across her sight, their white wings effortless. The sun burned on her wet shoulders and dazzled her eyes.

'Come in now,' said Alex, reappearing at her side. 'You'll get tired.'

She obeyed him, as she had obeyed him for the last three months, following the black head as it moved through the water and wading after him up the pink sands.

Alex had brought down an enormous flower-blazoned beach towel which he began spreading over the sand. Flinging himself down on it, he lay on his back, his hands under his head, staring at the sky.

She reluctantly lay down beside him, conscious of his breathing, the rise and fall of the muscled chest, the faint movements of his head as he settled more comfortably.

Closing her eyes she tried to think but all thought had been stilled inside her weeks ago. She slid into light sleep.

'Time to go in,' Alex said above her, waking her.

Her lids fluttered back and she looked up to find his face leaning over her. He wasn't looking at her own face, though, he was staring at the relaxed golden body in the tiny yellow bikini, and Sophie's heart stopped and beat with sickening speed again as he slowly reached out a long brown hand to touch her.

She couldn't move. The cool dry fingers wandered down the soft curve of her hip and caressed her bare thigh, slid inward so that she tensed and sprang up on a reflex protest.

Alex lifted his black head. A sardonic little smile touched his mouth. He didn't say a word but his hand returned and stroked her inner thigh again, his eyes holding hers as he touched her intimately, possessively, forcing her to accept the contact.

Sophie's eyes closed against the deep hypnotic stare of his eyes. She was shaking, shivering as though with cold, despite the deep heat of the sun overhead.

Alex's sudden movement made her eyes flick open again but by then she was forced back on to the towel, her whole body oppressed by the hard hot pressure of his, his lips hungrily draining hers as his kiss demanded her surrender.

The cool control with which he had behaved only moments ago was gone. She felt his heart thudding against her, heard the thick rasp of his breathing as he pushed one hand beneath her body to lift her towards him while the other hand slid strokingly from her shoulder to her thigh. Then the thin yellow bikini top slipped away and Alex buried his face between her bared breasts. 'Sophie,' he muttered hoarsely, his breathing warm on her white skin.

The dull passivity which had held for months was dissolving in the fierce heat of his caresses. Sophie lay weakly under him, her lips trembling in a yielding sigh, then her hands lifted to touch the sand-dusted brown shoulders, run over them exploringly to close behind his black head.

Her senses reeled under the pressure of the desire he was awaking in her. When his mouth closed over hers again she returned the kisses heatedly, her fingers thrusting into the damp hair, feeling the stiff tension in the muscles of his neck as she touched him.

Suddenly he moved away, breaking off the kiss so suddenly she was breathless. He wrapped her like a child in the beach towel and picked her up. Sophie came back to reality with a fierce realisation.

Alex moved up through the gardens, walking fast, his long legs covering the ground as though he were desperate to get to the house. Sophie caught the exotic flash of colour from the bougainvilleas and hibiscus massed for effect around the villa, felt the sun dazzling her eyes, then she was in the shadowy interior of the house and Alex's urgent, trembling hands were unwrapping her like an eagerly awaited present.

A wild panic started inside her. She backed away from the hungry possessive eyes as they ran over her body, shaking her head, beginning to tremble violently.

'No! Please, Alex, don't make me now,' she begged like a frightened child, her lip quivering, and saw blazing rage come into his hard face.

'Damn you to hell, you little cheat,' he bit out savagely through his teeth, the arrogant mouth going white with temper. 'You wanted me just now. Don't lie to me!' His hands shot out, shaking with a desire to punish and hurt, digging into her bare golden shoulders, his eyes glaring into hers as if he hated her enough to kill her.

Suddenly he flung her backwards. Her head swam with a sort of vertigo, unbalanced, blind. She fell across the bed and her eyes looked up in helpless panic as Alex's body forced itself down on her, his long rough thigh thrust between her legs, his mouth searching for hers and taking it with all the savagery she could see in his grey eyes.

Her struggle against him was brief, but any hope she might have nursed that he would offer her tenderness or gentleness would have been cruelly disillusioned. The powerful body imposed itself without a shred of concern, ignoring her harsh cry of pain. She caught the brief flash of the grey eyes as he threw her a glance, knew he had seen and been delighted by the icy panic on her face, and then Alex drove blindly for his own satisfaction, holding her shoulders down on the bed, breathing as though each breath might be his last, dragging air into his lungs hoarsely.

Shivering, aching, Sophie lay under him and listened to the sharp, fierce moans of pleasure a moment later, hating him. His black head collapsed against her breasts. He lay shuddering on her and she felt his mouth moving on the smooth white curve of her body.

After a long moment he lifted his head. His face was burning, his skin dark and hot, his eyes restless. She felt them searching her white face and met them bitterly, not hiding her sick reaction to his possession of her body.

Alex's bones clenched in on themselves, his mouth hardened. 'It needn't have been like that,' he said almost contemptuously. 'You made me go crazy. No man likes to see a woman cringe away from him.'

'No woman wants to have a man treat her like an animal,' Sophie cried in a shaking voice.

'I treated you the way you forced me to treat you,' Alex said in a cold, hard voice. 'If you'd given yourself it would all have been different.'

'I'll never give myself to you,' Sophie retorted, white and shivering.

His eyes lit with that icy rage that made his face totally dangerous, the strong jaw assertive, the mouth tight and bitter. 'Then I'll take you,' he promised. 'Every time I want you.' His eyes ran down over her in a scornful movement of cold desire. 'As often as I like. Your body gives me pleasure and it belongs to me.'

He rolled away from her and lay on his side, his face averted from her, his breathing gradually becoming normal. Sophie looked at the long golden line of his back, the fine short hairs marking that spine. A strange prickle of sexual awareness made the hair on the back of her neck rise. She hurriedly looked away, sliding off the other side of the bed and finding a short towelling robe into which she hurriedly tied herself.

Alex turned on to his back to watch her. She felt his stare but refused to meet it.

'Where do you think you're going?' he demanded.

'To have a shower,' Sophie said bitingly. 'I feel unclean.'

There was silence which made her skin turn cold. Alex came off the bed and she had a terrified impulse to run. She knew her impulsive insult had made his temper rise again. As she turned in panic, he swung her round and his hand stung across her face.

She gasped in shock, tears springing into her eyes, trembling. Alex looked at her, his face even whiter than her own. He stared at the dark hot mark glowing on her face. She saw his teeth bite into his lower lip and a red spot of blood showed there.

'You shouldn't have said that,' he accused in a low, shaking voice. 'My God, do you want to drive me completely out of my mind?'

Sophie stared at him, tears running down her face, and after a moment he flung away from her and went out, slamming the door after him with a violence that made the windows rattle.

She walked into the shower room and turned on the spraying jet, letting the cleansing water rinse away her fear and guilt. She had been passive, if not responsive, beneath Alex's complete domination, and she hated herself now for that. The five long years during which she had slept in a romantic dream of Simon had been dissolved in a few moments by the compelling rape of her body.

When she had dried herself, she took some time to dress, before lying down on her bed in the blue-shadowed room, trying not to think, trying not to feel, yet unable to stop her anguished thoughts from going over what Alex had done to her. The savage possession of her body had left too many marks, visible and invisible.

Deliberately she made herself think about Simon but her mind could not hold images of him. They blurred and evaporated. All she could think about was the driving movements of that powerful body, the moaned ecstasy of his voice.

She shivered and trembled as if she were in the grip of fever. His threat came back to haunt her. He had no intention of leaving her alone despite her open rejection, perhaps because of her open rejection. That was going to happen again. And again. Sophie rolled on to her face and let her tears soak into the pillow.

She could not bear it. She was no longer the same person who had clung to Simon that night in the conservatory. Alex had changed her by some chemical process she did not understand. The violent hatred and rejection she felt made no difference. When he held her down and took her with that remorseless savagery, he had done more than possess her body. He had possessed her mind.

Feelings are fragile, tenuous things which can snap or strengthen out of sight in the emotional hothouse which the heart provides. Sophie did not imagine that her heart had been touched by Alex Lefkas, but she could not force him out of her mind. He had been dominating her thoughts for the last three months, the threat of his possession permanently in her head, and now he had taken possession and his dark image smouldered inside her like a Byzantine icon in a shadowed corner.

Once only Simon had held her in that addictive memory; her body, heart and mind entirely his to command. Now Alex had her body and her mind and her heart was lost in a troubled limbo of confused emotions.

The door snapped open. 'What the hell are you doing sulking in here?'

She rubbed her fists into her wet eyes like a sad child before she got up and turned to face him.

Alex observed her muted unhappiness with an icy stare. His grey eyes flicked to the cheek he had struck. The mark had faded now, but she felt the heat in her skin returned as he looked at it.

'Dinner should be ready soon,' he said coolly. 'We'll have a drink first.'

She followed him into the long, white room which had a Moorish look, the primitive arches and pillars simple. Sophie sank down on to the deep-cushioned red couch and Alex poured her a Martini before getting himself some Scotch.

'Let's have some music,' he said, shooting her a glance. 'Why don't you choose it?'

Sophie obediently looked through the racks of LPs and chose some Spanish guitar music which matched the room and the deep purple glaze of the sky beyond the terrace.

Alex had sat down when she went back to the couch, and Sophie resumed her seat, moving slightly as she felt the brush of his thigh against hers. She knew he looked at her, she felt the hardening of his eyes.

'One day we'll go out fishing,' he said, however, as though ignoring her faint movement away from him. 'When you get a few miles out you can sometimes see flying fish. You ought to see some while we're here. They're one of the sights of the islands.'

'I'd like to,' Sophie said huskily.

'We could go dancing one night, too,' he said. 'There are a few good hotels on the island, although they're rather crowded just now.'

Sophie looked down into her pale, straw-coloured

drink. She lifted it to her mouth and the ice clinked against the glass.

They were here for two weeks. Time stretched and concertinaed depending on whether one was happy or miserable. Sophie had a sinking feeling that these were going to be the longest two weeks of her life.

The music behind them strummed rhythmically, rising to a fierce and pulsing crescendo, which began to weave itself into her blood, making her pulses quiver and burn. She felt Alex move and involuntarily looked round at him, her green eyes wide, disturbed. The brooding intensity of his stare intensified her own nervousness.

He suddenly looked away, his mouth tightening into a hard line. 'While we're here, Mama is having all the presents shipped to New York,' he told her. 'I thought we'd have them stored until we've decided where we want to live. My New York apartment may not suit you.'

Sophie could not see herself demanding somewhere better. Quietly she said, 'I don't mind where we live.'

He ignored that. 'There's no hurry for you to choose a place. You can look round at your leisure. I have a couple running my present place who we could keep on, if you like them. They've been with me for years. Mama found them. They're immigrants from Cos—they have a son who's just got into the organisation, but he is about to be married himself.'

She listened while he told her about the family, nodding, sensing that Alex was doing his best to re-establish a sort of calm between them.

'Your sister might like to come out and stay for a while,' Alex suggested. 'During her next vacation. I thought, in fact, we could have a family Christmas with Mama and your family, so that they could really get to know one another.'

Dinner was announced with broad smile from the tall,

curly-haired husband who was in charge of the garden
but who doubled as a butler when Alex was in residence,
wearing with obvious enjoyment the silk-lapelled white
jacket and trousers which matched which were, Alex
told her later, George's idea of a butler's livery. His
wife, Ava, did the cooking and her sister Juliet the
cleaning. It was, Sophie discovered, a family affair.
They all lived in a bungalow in the villa grounds. At first
she was to wonder how many of them there were—there
seemed at least a dozen. But in time she was able to sort
out the smiling faces as three generations of one family.
Even the youngest, Ava's son Gary, worked on the
estate. Seven years old and usually only wearing brief
well-washed shorts, he helped his father in the garden in
a lazy, unhurried fashion, pausing for constant rests in
the hot sun.

'When none of us are here, the place is theirs,' Alex
said drily. 'They are indulgent enough to let us come
now and then, but there's never any doubt as to who
runs the villa. I wouldn't even care to suggest which
flowers George should pick for the dinner table.'

The dinner was elaborately served and meltingly well
cooked, and Sophie wished her appetite was better. Under
Alex's watchful grey eyes she picked at the food, tasting
sweet potatoes and baked bananas for the first time, lik-
ing them but feeling so little hunger that she had to force
herself to eat merely to please Ava and George.

They took their coffee in the cool sitting-room with
the sound of insects and frogs filling the warm night
beyond the open windows. The servants left for their
bungalow. The villa was deserted. Sophie sat with dry
lips and a trembling body, hardly daring to look at
Alex. He played a Ravel recording, the wild discordant
crash of the music suiting the mood she felt in him. No,
she thought, gritting her teeth, he can't. Not again. She

didn't look at him but, every antenna in her body picked
it up from him, the submerged throb of passion beating
beneath the surface of his masked features.

Lighting a cigar, he stared at the white arches of the
room, blowing wreaths of smoke slowly towards them.
His body relaxed gracefully, he listened to the music, but
there was no relaxation in his hidden thoughts. When he
got up to turn off the music centre which was housed behind a softly smoked wall of glass along one wall, Sophie
watched him with wary intensity.

Shielding her eyes with her lids, she pretended to yawn.
'I'm tired,' she said huskily. 'I think I'm still suffering
from that journey.'

Alex laughed derisively. She flicked a quick, nervous
look at him through her lashes. He moved back towards
her and she stood up, stiffening as he took her arms in
his hands.

The sardonic eyes watched her until she looked at him.
Alex smiled slowly, mockingly. 'Come to bed, Sophie,'
he whispered, and she was too frightened of the barbaric
outburst she had provoked last time she tried to resist him
to try to refuse him this time.

The chilled white wine she had drunk with her dinner
had helped to cloud her mind a little, but as if Alex
sensed that she was still stiff with panic, he suddenly
turned away, went to the brandy decanter and poured her
a double brandy. When he put it into her hand she looked
at it and then at him.

'Drink it,' he said in a low voice.

Sophie put it reluctantly to her mouth. Alex watched
her until the glass was empty, until a slow flush crept into
her face as the brandy entered her bloodstream.

She followed him into her bedroom. Someone had been
in and tidied the ruffled bed, she realised, glancing at it.

She could imagine what the servants must have thought and her face flushed more deeply.

Alex was looking at her, his grey eyes narrowed. His arm went round her and she felt him slide her zip down. Trembling, she stood like a child while he slowly stripped her, his eyes moving over her unresisting body, a slow hard flush growing on his cheekbones.

His hand tilted her chin and he looked down into her wide, glazed eyes.

'You're beautiful,' he muttered. His mouth parted on a strange low sigh. 'Sophie, don't fight me tonight.'

She stared at the parted, sensual line of his mouth. It came closer. Before it touched her, her lips were opening to his kiss. He deepened the exploration of her mouth and her hands crept up his chest to fold around his neck. She felt the warm soothing stroke of his fingertips run down her spine, follow the rounded curve of her body and then slide up to encompass her naked breasts.

Sophie's moan of pleasure broke out of her without her having known it. Alex tensed and lifted his head to look at her flushed face, the closed eyes, the parted mouth.

She was not even aware of the sharp triumphant groan he gave. Her heart was deafening her to everything but a burning desire which was consuming her ability to think.

Once, as they lay in the bed, twisting in unsated excitement, she surfaced long enough to know it was happening to her, to understand the fevered hunger Alex had unleashed from her body, and then his mouth closed round her breast again and she sank without a struggle back into the warm, dark seas of sexual satisfaction.

Alex cried out her name on a thick moan of pleasure just once, piercing her abject submission, but far from hating him for the triumphant note in his voice, she ran her trembling hands over his black head, holding him against her, answering him. 'Oh, Alex, Alex,' she groaned as his mouth covered her own again.

When they drifted into sleep she was held in his arms, her head on his shoulder, their bodies still tangled together.

Sophie woke up to feel sunlight dancing over her lids. She moved, reluctant, her body aching strangely, and then felt the alien naked flesh curved round her own and opened her eyes on a startled, shaken reflex.

Alex was leaning on his elbow, his chin on his hand, watching her. His other hand lay calmly and possessively on her smooth naked thigh.

Hot, betraying colour surged up her face. She looked away, biting her lip.

He laughed softly. 'Kiss me,' he commanded arrogantly, his eyes fixed on her averted face.

When she didn't move he lifted his hand to her chin and turned her face towards him, kissing her lingeringly.

'I'm hungry,' he said as he moved away. She gave him a startled look and he began to laugh, huskily, softly.

'No, no, my darling—for food, not love.' His eyes took on a wicked amusement as her flushed face grew more confused. 'Although, if you tempted me,' he insinuated in that husky voice, smiling, then with a sudden change of mood swung off the bed. Sophie hurriedly turned her eyes from the lean muscled body as he walked across the room.

'I'll see you later,' Alex promised, amusement in his voice. He went out and Sophie stretched, abruptly excited and feeling the warm languor of the night before enveloping her again. Alex had hurt and exalted her, driven her mad with pleasure, forced her to give him back the sensual urgency he was offering her, and Sophie could not regret what had happened. She hadn't guessed her body was capable of a pleasure so consuming, so satisfactory. She felt too lazy to move, stretching the warm curve of her body like a sleepy cat. Sunlight dappled the room and gave her skin a flickering patina. She heard Alex whistling in his room and her mouth curved. If she didn't get up she guessed he would come in and make fun of her. Reluctantly she slid out of the bed and went to shower.

They spent the whole day on the beach, sunning and swimming, talking sleepily now and then, feeling no need to do anything. When the sun went down with that abrupt and startling rush, they ate dinner and then listened to music exactly as they had the previous evening. Sophie sat beside Alex, her thigh resting warmly against his, conscious of his every look, every movement. She was waiting for the music to end, for the sweet pulsing excitement to begin again, and Alex knew. The lazy mockery of his grey eyes caressed her body and smiled into her eyes.

It was a pattern which was to become fixed as their honeymoon went on—days spent in the sun and the blue water, nights spent in each other's arms, the same warm lazy rhythm possessing all the motions of time, so that Sophie lost all sense of awareness and was merely possessed by the heated magic Alex had spun around her.

They went deep-sea fishing in a fast sleek white boat and Sophie leaned on the rail, watching the creaming wake following them, gasping with delight at the flying fish Alex pointed out to her. Sunlight glittered in rainbow brilliance on their scales as they leapt from the water and vanished again and Alex grinned down into Sophie's excited green eyes. 'Fantastic, aren't they?'

'Marvellous,' she breathed.

She brought him a drink later and he kissed her hand as he took the glass, the caress of his sideways glance making her heart quicken.

When the fish he was fighting with escaped Sophie gave a cheer and Alex chased her along the deck, holding her, squirming, kissing her. 'Impudent little bitch,' he whispered, his lips brushing her nose. The crew watched, their grins a flash of white teeth in deeply tanned faces.

'You're supposed to sympathise with me, not the fish,' Alex ordered.

She flicked her long lashes down. 'Yes, sir.'

He squeezed her waist, making her shriek. 'That tickles—don't!'

Remorselessly he did it again, roaring with amusement at her wild protests. The sun and wind was deepening their tan, too, their bodies a uniform smooth gold which was becoming something akin to teak. Sophie felt freer than she had ever felt in her life, physical satisfaction and relaxation changing her whole outlook.

Several times they dined at a modern hotel a few miles from the villa, staying to dance and watch the cabaret after their meal. Moving around the tiny floor in Alex's arms, Sophie watched the black head turn as a woman in a low-cut black gown walked swayingly towards a table. There was amused appreciation in his grey eyes and to her horror Sophie felt an appalling stab of jealousy. It was such a physical feeling that she winced and drew in her breath, and Alex looked down at her with his brows jerking together.

'What's wrong?' He took in her whitened face, the tremble of her body, and his eyes darkened anxiously. 'You're not feeling ill? That lobster—I told you shell-fish could be a risk!'

Dazedly she shook her head. 'I've got a headache,' she lied. 'Do you mind if we go?'

'Of course not,' Alex said at once, guiding her back to their table. 'Why didn't you say something? I never noticed you were off colour.'

They drove back to the villa and Sophie sat in the dark car, her body shivering. Why hadn't she realised before? He had taken possession of her so gradually that she had not understood what was happening. His dark image had supplanted Simon in the beginning because she was so afraid of him that she could think of nothing and nobody else. He had established a foothold in her mind through sheer terror. The months while she waited for her wedding day had been drugged oblivion of everything but Alex and her fear of what he intended.

The second stage of his conquest had come when he forced her body with that ruthless determination. She had hated him, but as he entered her body, he had also been finalising his possession of her mind, and her own helpless surrender to him later had been the last stage of his campaign against her.

She had been blind not to see that mere physical possession would not be enough to satisfy his raging thirst for revenge. She had offended that powerful male ego in its deepest stronghold. It would never have been enough for Alex to possess her body—he had wanted her mind, her heart, as well. He wanted all that she had once given Simon. She could remember him saying so, his eyes savage. 'Everything in you,' he had said.

Now she miserably recognised that Alex had got his desire. She had been sick with jealousy as he glanced at another woman. How or when it had happened to her she had no idea. She had never admitted even to herself at the start that she found him attractive—but now she bent her bright head, shuddering, and admitted it silently. It was why Alex had several times wrung a response out of her even when she still loved Simon. The five long empty years when she had been possessed by a memory had been a mirage. She had lived on a kiss, a look, and they had never been enough.

Her love for Simon had been kept alive like a tiny cherished flame. It had all been an illusion. Alex had exploded the myth as he forced her body that afternoon in the shadows of her bedroom.

The illusory love had been almost dead by then, anyway, she realised. Alex's hovering threat had seen to that, supplanting Simon's image with his own, making her think of him rather than her absent lover, so that she had found it harder and harder to remember Simon's face.

She glanced sideways secretly at Alex's absorbed dark face. I love him, she thought. He must never know. At all costs I've got to hide it from him. Alex wanted the triumph of completely defeating her, and she must not concede him that desired victory.

In the villa Alex followed her into her room with a glass of water and some pills, insisting that she take them, frowning anxiously at her pale face. 'Get some sleep, darling. I hope you haven't had too much sun. It is just a headache?'

She smiled, a pale movement of her mouth. 'Yes, just a headache.'

He held her face between his palms, kissing her lingeringly. 'Poor darling, you look so tired. Goodnight, Sophie.'

When he had gone she got into bed and lay in the darkness with a haunting conviction of disaster. Alex wasn't a safe man to love; his past life warned her of that. The sophisticated, experienced mind was used to a frequent change of scene and women. It hadn't occurred to her until now that the possibility of Alex being faithful to her was remote, but now she winced and moaned under her breath as she faced it. She would not be able to bear it if she found out he was having other women.

Sophie looked into the future and found it an intolerable blank.

CHAPTER TEN

SHE found New York intimidating. Her months in Crete and then at the quiet villa fronting the coral sands had increased her dislike of city life, so that she winced from the roar of traffic, the countless outbursts of sound which surrounded one in the crowded streets. There always seemed to be men at work, drilling, shouting, making the air hellish around them. Streams of cars choked the roads. Jostling armies of office workers pushed their way around the blocks.

'Back to real life, I'm afraid,' Alex said drily as she turned to him from the wide high window of his apartment.

What did that mean? she wondered, her secret glance disturbed. Now that their honeymoon was over would his passionate concentration on her lapse into the indifference of sated conquest?

'You can start looking for somewhere else if you don't like this place,' Alex told her.

She gave a brief shrug. 'I'm quite happy with it. It's convenient for you, isn't it?'

The grey eyes flicked oddly at her and his mouth twisted. 'Are you saying you don't give a damn where we live?' There was a cold, barbed hostility in the tone.

'I don't know New York yet,' Sophie protested. 'Wouldn't it be wisest if we waited until I knew which part of it I preferred?'

Alex surveyed her coolly. 'I thought you might want to get a place outside the City—somewhere close enough for me to drive in when I came to the office but far enough out for you to have a semblance of peace. There are plenty of places around the city where we could get a suitable property.'

'Whatever you like,' Sophie shrugged.

'Don't be so damned dutiful!' His snap made her flush and look at him nervously.

'And don't look at me like that,' he said harshly.

'How do you want me to look at you?' Sophie's heart beat faster as she asked the question in a husky voice.

Alex turned away, his dark brows drawn. 'Mama says she's coming for a few days next week,' he told her.

Sophie was delighted. 'That's wonderful! It will be so nice to see her.'

Alex glanced over his shoulder at the lit pleasure of her face and his eyes were expressionless. 'Yes,' he said drily.

She discovered as he resumed his working life that the glimpses she had had of his energy and dedication had not given her a true picture of just how much of him went into his work. He rose very early each morning, left for his office before Sophie was more than half awake, came home sometimes for dinner, just as often dining out and returning very late. Sophie hid the pain and jealousy she felt beneath a cool mask. He always said he was with business acquaintances; executives of the company or foreign clients. She did not know how true it was and she had no intention of allowing him to see how much she was possessed by a fear that he was already seeing other women.

Sophie gave dinner parties for his friends and for executives from the firm. She learnt to play the society hostess, taking great care with menus, dressing the part to perfection, learning how to steer a drifting conversation, how to listen and smile so that the men talking to her imagined they were fascinating her. She realised that it was not necessary to say much. A man who has talked freely while a beautiful woman smiles and watches him with apparent admiration is a man who has had a wonderful evening. She was told so over and over again. Alex would listen, his dark brows level, while one of their guests praised Sophie to him enthusiastically. It amused her that they would always say the same thing. 'I thoroughly enjoyed our little chat. Your wife is as witty as she's beautiful, Alex.' Wit, she discovered, consisted not of what you said but of how well you listened and laughed.

The mask she had pulled over her face for Alex sufficed for his friends. Cool, smiling, poised, she went through the motions of her life while Alex watched her without comment.

The one thing that eased her jealous anxiety was the fact that Alex made love to her with a passion that showed no sign of slackening. He never uttered words of love, but his desire for her burnt as high as it had during their honeymoon. She learnt to recognise the narrowed, intense stare with which he watched her and to know what was in his mind. It was not only Sophie who could not wait to push their guests out of the apartment.

In early December she caught a ferocious cold, shivering convulsively in the icy winter. New York was wrapped in a blanket of crystal snow which hardened under the feet of passers-by, turning the streets to skating rinks. Alex insisted on having a doctor to confirm that all she had was a cold and Sophie was put to bed and told firmly to stay there. Alex was about to take a brief trip to Australia, which Sophie had intended to make with him. Alex had insisted she should come, but now it was out of the question. He came into her bedroom to sit on the side of her bed and smile at her, brushing the ruffled lock of golden hair back from her deeply flushed face.

'Just stay in bed until I get back,' he said. 'I'll be gone for four days. By the time I get back I'll expect you to have got rid of the cold.' His grey eyes mocked her. 'Then I'll join you in the bed,' he promised, laughing at her.

As he bent towards her she turned her face away. 'No, you mustn't kiss me. You'll catch my cold.'

Alex halted, watching her. He picked up her hand and kissed the palm, his mouth warm on her damp skin. 'Try to miss me,' he said huskily, then went out with abrupt movements, while she stared at her closed door and felt tears rising to her eyes.

What had he meant by that? She yearned to believe that Alex really cared for her. He veered between that sardonic watchfulness and a gentle tenderness which she found deeply moving, but she dared not let herself believe Alex felt anything but desire for her, because the pain of finding out she was wrong would be too destructive.

She stayed in bed, nursed with devotion by Rhea, the small dark housekeeper, dosed with hot fresh lemon and aspirin, her appetite tempted by delicate little meals which Rhea took great trouble over. Sophie enjoyed tempting Rhea to sit beside her bed and talk about Cos, her home, watching the sparkling black eyes and listening to the fast deep Greek. 'But I must get on,' Rhea would wail, half rising. 'I must not keep you with my chatter, Madame.' Sophie would laugh and pat her hand. 'Stay and tell me about the Easter festival again,' knowing that Rhea loved talking about the green, fertile hills and valleys of her homeland. Although Cos had little to offer in the way of archaeological sites, it had a beauty which lingered in Rhea's mind and made Sophie wonder if she wouldn't be much happier if she returned there. When she asked Rhea, though, the woman shrugged philosophically. 'There, my husband was poor. Here, we are rich.' She enjoyed the luxury of her surroundings, the good food and wine she could have every day. She was not prepared to sacrifice them for a return to Cos. That was a dream which sweetened her life here, but it was just that—a dream.

Everyone has dreams, Sophie thought, lying in her bed and waiting impatiently for Alex to come back to her. Dreams which are fulfilled are rare and perhaps, when that happens, we have to find another dream to take the place of the one we have achieved. We can't live without our dreams.

She was deeply disappointed when Alex rang to say he could not get back as planned. 'It's taking longer than I'd anticipated,' he told her flatly. 'I'm sorry. Another two days at least, I'm afraid.'

'It doesn't matter,' Sophie said politely, feeling him very far away, his voice calm and distant.

'Is your cold better?'

'Much,' she said. 'Rhea has been nursing me with lemon every two hours.'

When he had rung off, she lay wondering if it was really business which was keeping him. Had he met someone? Agony stabbed inside her and she put her hands over her face. She would never know, but these recurring fears were making her life hell.

She got up next day, although she did not risk going out in the icy winter weather, spending the day by the circular brick fireplace in the middle of the vast lounge. An electric log fire glowed under the copper hood. Centrally heated though it was, the winter onslaught made additional heat welcome in the apartment. During the late afternoon she read a detective story with a tape of muted music in the background. The sky beyond the windows lowered gloomily. She had a horrible feeling that more snow was on the way.

When the phone rang Rhea answered it and came to her to tell her it was her mother. Sophie lifted the receiver, smiling. 'Hallo, Mum.'

She usually rang her mother—knowing the expense of transatlantic calls was too much for the small family budget. Sophie had got into the habit of ringing once a week, knowing her mother looked forward to the calls.

Today, though, her mother was urgently distressed. 'Sophie, your father has had a heart attack.'

Sophie whitened. 'No! Oh, Mum—how? What happened? How is he?'

'It isn't serious,' Mrs Bryant said with a sob in her voice. 'Oh, I was frightened, Sophie. It was this morning, just after he got up, I didn't understand what was happening and he looked so awful. They took him to hospital and they say it's a minor attack. He'll recover, they say, but oh, Sophie, it's been such a shock!'

Sophie talked soothingly to her, said she was coming at once. Mrs Bryant sighed. 'Can you? I'd be grateful if you could. Patsy is at college and I feel so alone. Alex won't mind?'

'He isn't here, he's in Australia,' Sophie told her. 'I'll leave him a note.'

When her mother had rung off, Sophie called Rhea and explained what had happened, said she was going to England as soon as she could get a plane. She and Rhea packed a case. Sophie rang the airport and got a seat on the next flight to London, then she was driven to the airport. She had written a brief note for Alex, explaining about her father's attack. Rhea's husband, Theo, drove her to the airport and carried her case for her to the desk. She had a foreboding of alarm as she looked at the grey sky. Would the plane take off in this weather? She did not much like the idea of spending hours in a blizzard in the airport lounge.

To her relief, the flight took off only an hour late and the sky had still not released the sagging dark clouds hanging over the city. Snow was up there, icing the atmosphere, but they were lucky that the flight took off before it fell.

London was so much warmer that Sophie felt over-heated in her heavy mink coat as she walked off the plane at Heathrow. The sky was a pale wintry grey, but a watery sun was struggling to get through the clouds and the fields were misty in the distance.

She was driven to her parents' house, her discarded coat beside her, her slender body elegant in a dark green trouser suit, the white cowled sweater beneath it warm enough for English weather. She had slept on the long flight. The early morning mist was rising all round her as the green fields of Kent flashed past.

Mrs Bryant had tears in her eyes as she hugged her. 'Thank you for coming, darling. Patsy's here too. You're good girls, both of you.'

'Aren't we?' Patsy teased, coming up to grin at Sophie over her mother's shoulders. 'Saintly, both of us!'

Their mother laughed, brushing her tears aside with one hand. 'Oh, you're a tease, Patsy. It does help to have you both here. That's what I meant.'

'Get the kettle on and stop making us feel silly,' Patsy mocked. She stretched out a hand for Sophie's coat. 'Wow, that's what I call a coat! Alex certainly spoils you. Can I try it on?'

She was already sliding her arms into it and Sophie said drily: 'Help yourself.'

Patsy's small firm figure was lost in the elegant folds and she made a wry face. 'I'm too short for it. Let's see you in it. Come on, model it for me.'

Sophie obediently put it on and Patsy and her mother watched her delightedly, smiling. Patsy's bright chatter was designed, Sophie recognised, to calm their mother's anxiety and make her feel that everything was normal. Mrs Bryant had told Sophie as she arrived that her father was picking up, his condition stabilising. 'He's been lucky,' she had told her. 'But now he must take things easily, they say.

'It was a warning,' she had added later, and the worry of the last two days had left grim lines in her usually contented face.

'You just don't know how lucky you are,' Patsy said lightly. 'A mink coat and Alex too!'

Sophie laughed and dropped the coat casually over a chair. Patsy snatched it up, smoothed the fur enviously.

'When shall I be able to see Dad?' Sophie asked her mother. 'Have you seen him?'

'They let me in for five minutes, but for the moment he can't have any other visitors,' her mother answered quietly. She poured the tea and handed Sophie a cup. 'When does Alex get back from Australia?'

'I'm not sure,' Sophie said. 'Tomorrow or the next day—it depends on how his business goes. It was taking longer than he'd expected.'

'What's New York like?' Patsy asked, sipping her tea.

'Why not come and find out?' Sophie invited, smiling at her. 'Alex thought we could have a family Christmas this year.' Her face sobered. 'If Dad's well enough to travel.'

Mrs Bryant sighed. 'I doubt that, Sophie. I really doubt that. It would be too soon.'

When Mrs Bryant came back from the hospital the following day, she looked much happier, her eyes quite hopeful. 'I had a quarter of an hour with him today. He's out of the oxygen tent and he could talk a little bit. His colour is still awful, but he looks more like himself than he did.'

It was news which cheered them all up and Sophie insisted on taking Patsy and her mother out to dinner at a hotel in Canterbury that evening. Mrs Bryant was able to relax now that the worst of her anxiety was over. Sophie kept her amused by telling her about New York, the villa at which she and Alex had spent their honeymoon, the emerald pendant Alex had given her on their return to New York afterwards.

Patsy put out her tongue. 'Stop making me jealous! Mink coats and emeralds—and I have to budget to buy a new pair of jeans!'

Her envy was largely assumed to amuse their mother, but Sophie smiled at her. 'When you come to stay I'll look out for a handsome millionaire for you.'

'Bald and at least sixty,' Patsy said. 'Then he'll die on our honeymoon and leave me a fabulously wealthy widow.'

'Patsy!' Mrs Bryant scolded, shaking her head, laughing.

Sophie got into bed that night wondering if Alex had yet heard the news. She had tried to ring him in Sydney before she left and he had not been available. She had half expected him to ring her all day, but there had been no word from him. What was he doing in Australia? Was he too engrossed in a pursuit of someone else to be bothered to ring her? Aching, angry, miserable, she tried to get to sleep and found it hard. When she did fall asleep her head was thudding and she felt like death.

The next morning Mrs Bryant and Patsy went shopping together, leaving Sophie alone because her head still ached from the sleepless night she had had. Deciding fresh air would improve the way she felt, she walked down the road and turned through the little wicket gate which led into the park of Dancing Court. As a child she had often walked here. The house was visible through the trees, the white outline marking the grey sky.

Sophie kept her distance from it, not wishing to see any of the family. The damp grass was littered with drenched leaves. The dark branches rustled in the wind as she walked beneath them. Sheep turned mild, startled eyes on her and stared after her.

Suddenly she heard a twig crack and her heart skidded. She moved behind a wide-barrelled oak, trying to merge with the dark trunk, guessing already who she would see and hoping that if she kept still he might not notice her.

He walked past, his hands in his pockets, his fair head bent. From her hiding place she watched him and felt a wrung compassion for the tired grimness of his face.

Suddenly he stopped dead. His head lifted as though he felt her presence, could sense it.

Sophie bit her lip, feeling oddly sick.

Simon's head swung, his eyes searched the crowding skeletal trees. They halted and she knew he had seen her. He looked at her as he had never looked at her before—distantly, assessingly.

'Hallo,' he said, as he might to a stranger. 'I heard you'd flown over. How's your father now?'

She put a hand on the ribbed dark trunk to steady herself, her skin cold, her nerves jumpy. 'Much better, thank you.' She needed the contact with the tree to make this real, to assure herself that she really stood here talking to Simon in this unreal fashion.

He looked somehow different. Time had made small changes in him which had altered the blue eyes, the weary look of his features.

'I'm glad to hear that,' he said. His eyes moved up to the grey sky. 'Not a bad day, is it?'

'It's snow-bound in New York.' The ludicrous small talk made her want to laugh, but she was in no mood for laughter. Her brain had atrophied. She couldn't think.

'Really? They always seem to get snow in winter. I've only been there in the summer.'

'Very wise,' Sophie said drily.

It was difficult even to say that much. Simon was a stranger, withdrawn from her. All the passion, the need, she had once felt had gone, perhaps had gone long ago without her realising it, sunk into the emptiness of the years when they never saw each other. The habit of love covered the emptiness within, disguised the hollow nature of a passion she had thought inextinguishable.

'How's Lucy?' she asked, and saw his face light up.

'She's fine, really fine. Doing very well at the school. They said that now she's accepted she can do it, she'll go on improving.'

'That's wonderful,' Sophie said, smiling at him. Simon had some love in his life, an emotion which made life worth living for him. Lucy had always mattered more to him than anything else. It had been for Lucy that he had made a desert of his emotional life and it was good that Lucy should be repaying him now by beginning to turn outwards at the world after years of a silent rejection.

'Elaine's in the Canaries,' he said. 'A holiday in the sun. She hates winter here.'

Sophie's eyes hardened. She made no comment on that. She looked down at the ground, pushed a toe into the damp grass, searching for a way of ending the conversation without rudeness.

She felt a movement and looked up in alarm. Simon took another step and she fell back against the tree, silently shaking her head at the look in his intent eyes.

'Just once, Sophie,' he muttered.

'Please, don't,' she begged, but he caught her face in his hands and dropped tiny pleading kisses on her closed mouth, murmuring her name.

'Sophie, oh, Sophie, how could you do it?'

Sophie wrenched herself away from him, her face very pale. 'Don't,' she muttered, and then she turned and ran down through the park, tears in her eyes.

She could not be angry with him. Simon's world was so empty. He had tried to hold her because he needed that distant unreachable dream, a star gleaming on his dark horizon. It had made life bearable for him. Simon had never asked what it did to her. She had spent five long years of her life needing him and it had all been a waste because Simon's love had not been real. Sophie was a woman, not a dream. She wanted more than to be worshipped and dreamt about.

That was why Alex had been able to reach into her crystal shell and shatter it, drag her out into his arms, make her give him the pent-up passion she had never been able to give Simon.

Looking back, she saw her feelings for Simon and could scarcely believe in them. Compared to the piercing heat of her desire for Alex they had no validity at all.

She got back to the house to find her mother and Patsy in the kitchen making the lunch. They looked at her, eyes bright, smiling.

'Alex is here! He's upstairs.'

Sophie's heart thudded. She turned and ran up the stairs and into her bedroom. Alex stood with his back to her at the window, the black head not moving. On the floor beside him lay an oval jeweller's box. Something in the set of his wide shoulders made Sophie halt, suddenly cold.

'Alex,' she said huskily, enquiringly.

'Enjoyed your walk?' He didn't turn and her eyes moved past him to the upward sweep of the park of Dancing Court. Sophie's eyes widened, her breath caught.

He turned then, his face icy and barbaric. 'You little

bitch,' he muttered. 'How often have you met him since you got here?'

'You saw,' she said weakly. He had watched her and Simon from here, seen their conversation among the oaks. Sophie began to tremble, remembering Simon's attempt to kiss her. What had Alex thought? Or could she guess?

'Oh, I saw,' he bit out.

'It was accidental, our meeting,' Sophie said nervously. 'I had a headache and went for a walk. I just happened to meet him.'

'Just happened to?' Alex's smile was derisive. 'The way you just happened to meet him in the conservatory that night?' He moved towards her, kicking the smooth blue box out of his way with an angry movement. 'I'm taking you back to New York tomorrow and from now on you don't go anywhere unless I'm with you.'

He put a hand under her chin and forced her head up, stared at her mouth, brought out a handkerchief and roughly wiped her lips. 'If you ever let him touch you again I'll kill you!'

Sophie looked at him, drowning in uncertainty and hope. He pushed her away, as though her stare infuriated him. Trembling, she looked down and her eye was caught by the box.

'What's that? Is it for me?'

He laughed grimly. 'Who else? I came flying over from Sydney like a besotted fool, only to see you in another man's arms.'

Sophie ran a nervous tongue over her dry lips. 'Aren't you going to give it to me?' The stammered lightness sounded false in her own ears and Alex gave her another of his cold hard smiles.

'Pick it up.'

She flushed at the tone, the words. He swung away and bent to pick up the box, unlatched the catch, shoved the open box into her hands. She caught her breath at the flashing brilliance of the stones.

'Oh, Alex!' she whispered.

He laughed harshly. 'I shall want more gratitude than that,' he told her with a biting savagery which was meant to cut into her. The grey eyes flicked to the bed and then back to her face. 'Much more,' he added sneeringly.

'Don't,' she muttered, wincing at the brutal desire in his face.

He drew a thick breath through his teeth. 'I ought to take you now to teach you who you belong to,' he muttered. 'I think you need some more lessons.' His voice deepened and rose. 'My God, I haven't been away from you for a week and I can't even trust you that long!'

Tears sprang into her eyes. She was shaking, white. 'Alex, don't, please don't be angry. I didn't even want to see him. I . . .'

'Don't lie to me—at least spare me that. I saw you in his arms up there. I've seen you kiss him before.' His lips twisted in a bitter tormented smile. 'Do you think I ever forget it? Do you think I can push the memory out of my head? Every time I have you in my arms I remember the way you kissed him and I want to kill you.'

She stared at him, her green eyes wide and feverish with hope. The shaking jealousy in his voice, in the flash of the grey eyes, was moving in her veins like adrenalin. Huskily, she said : 'I stopped loving Simon months ago.'

His body stiffened. The grey eyes searched her face. His cheekbones tautened and his mouth was held steady, only a flickering muscle beside it betraying any emotion.

'Just now I wasn't in his arms. He tried to kiss me and I wouldn't let him. I ran away. And I wasn't even tempted to stay for a second.'

Even at the risk of letting him see the hold he had over her heart and senses, she had to make him believe her because she could not bear to have him look at her with that icy contempt and hostility.

She would rather have Alex laugh in triumph and mockery as he realised how completely he possessed her, than have him hate her as he was doing now.

Alex was not laughing, though. He was moving closer to her, his face very pale. 'Are you telling the truth?'

She held his probing stare, nodding.

His hand curved round her cheek, the fingers stroking her skin. She silently moved her head and kissed his wrist where the stiff white cuff exposed the blue-veined strength of it.

Alex inhaled sharply. Sophie looked up at him nervously, her lashes flickering over her green eyes, her mouth trembling.

'Oh, God, my darling,' Alex whispered, pulling her into his arms. His lips moved over her hair as she clung to him, her hands stroking his long back. 'I love you desperately, Sophie.'

She closed her eyes, unable to speak, happiness making her tremble and feel almost sick.

Alex's arms tightened. 'You've got to learn to love me. I can't live without you. I need you.'

Her voice issued so drily from her lips that it was scarcely audible. 'I do love you.'

He held her away, searching her face with leaping, intent eyes. 'Sophie?'

Sophie's eyes looked passionately at him. Her mouth trembled. 'Alex darling,' she whispered. 'Oh, Alex darling!'

His mouth moved down urgently and she met it with unhidden eagerness, her arms laced round his neck, holding his head as the kiss deepened to a hungry passion which threatened to flare beyond their control. Alex's hands moved tremblingly over her. His heart pounded.

He was breathing with thick excitement.

'Lunch!' Patsy called from the foot of the stairs.

They broke apart, startled. Laughter rose in both of them. Alex yelled, 'Coming!' and they heard Patsy laughing as she went away.

'My God, I never felt less like food in my life.' Alex groaned wryly, grinning at her.

'We'll have to go down,' Sophie said, still laughing.

'I suppose so.' He sighed reluctantly. 'How long, my darling? How long have you known you loved me?'

'Since our honeymoon,' she said, grimacing.

His eyes widened. 'That long? My God, why didn't you tell me? You hid it from me all this time?'

'I didn't want to make a fool of myself,' Sophie said drily. 'I didn't think you loved me. You've never said you did.'

'I wasn't confessing the way I felt for you when I knew you loved another man,' he said grimly.

'You made such awful threats to me about what you were going to do to me when we were married,' said Sophie, her green eyes teasing.

He flushed. 'I had to force you to marry me. I suppose I half meant them. I was going crazy with jealousy at the time.'

Her face took on a startled disbelief. 'Did you love me then?'

'I think I fell in love with you at a very early stage,' he said with a sort of grim amusement. 'I just didn't recognise what was going on inside me. When you kept slapping me down, I told myself to forget you, but I couldn't. Then that morning in London when you called me a phoney and started crying, I knew. I wanted to crawl on my hands and knees to make you forgive me. I came down to Kent to start getting you to take me seriously—I meant then to marry you. I told my mother before I left how I left how I felt and she gave me her blessing.'

Sophie's eyes lit up with pleasure. 'Did she?'

'You know she adores you,' he said teasingly, smiling at her. 'She was delighted.' The smile went and his eyes darkened. 'Then I saw you with him and my world crashed down round my ears. I hadn't realised it was possible to feel such pain and not scream. I stood and watched you in his arms and I didn't make a sound. My cigar burnt down to my fingers. In a funny sort of way, the pain of my burnt skin was almost a relief.'

She leant her head on his wide shoulder. 'Oh, Alex darling—I'm sorry.'

'When I said I was going to marry you it was just said out of sheer rage with that bitch for the snide remarks about you being my mistress, but when I'd had time to think I realised I still wanted you. I was taking an appalling risk, marrying someone in love with another man, but I banked everything on the way I'd been able to get you to respond in London and then later outside your house that night. I didn't think then that you might love me, but I was prepared to live with that if I could have you in my bed every night.'

'Hedonist,' she muttered, half laughing, half horrified.

Alex made a wry face. 'I was kidding myself. I knew damned well it wasn't enough. However responsive you were, I wanted more. I wanted to be able to tell you how I felt and I had to shut it all inside me. Sometimes I thought I'd go mad. The sheer necessity of saying it aloud was driving me crazy.'

'And me,' she said shakily. Holding his dark head, she kissed him hungrily. 'I love you, Alex darling.'

He drew a long hard breath. 'And him?' His eyes searched hers.

'Nothing,' Sophie said huskily. 'Not a shred of it left. I had wondered how I would feel, seeing him again, and when I did it was like seeing a stranger. I felt sad, that's all. Poor Simon! He made me feel guilty, but that was the only feeling I had.'

Alex sighed deeply. 'I've dreaded the moment when you'd see him again. When I rang the apartment from Sydney and discovered you were over here, I almost went out of my mind. I knew you'd see him. I'd wanted to be here when that happened, to keep you apart. On the plane I was sweating with terror. Then I got here and you were out. I came up here and looked out of the window and saw you with him. When he started to kiss you I nearly went out to get a gun.' He laughed, but his eyes weren't amused.

'It didn't mean a thing,' said Sophie, kissing him. 'The lightest touch of your hand means more to me now than the most passionate kiss from Simon.'

The grey eyes ran over her like the touch of flame, branding her, burning his possession on her, and her body throbbed and pulsed with a need to have that ownership confirmed in physical assertion.

She felt that need in Alex too. His eyes slid sideways to the bed and his heart thudded as she rested on his body.

Patsy bellowed, 'What are you doing, you two? This food is getting cold. Come on, that can wait.'

Sophie began laughing. 'Damn her,' grinned Alex, laughing too, then he picked up the diamond necklace and deftly laced it round her throat, smiling at her as he stood back to admire it.

'That will knock Patsy's eyes out,' he said wickedly.

Hand in hand they went downstairs.

WHAT READERS SAY ABOUT
HARLEQUIN SUPERROMANCE #1

End of Innocence
by Abra Taylor

"I am impatiently awaiting the
next Superromance."
J.D.,* Sandusky, Ohio

"I couldn't put it down!"
M.M., North Baltimore, Ohio

"Just great—I can't wait until
the next one."
R.M., Melbourne, Florida

"I *loved* it!"
A.C., Pailin, New Jersey

"I enjoyed *End of Innocence*
by Abra Taylor so much."
J.L., Greenville, South Carolina

Harlequin Presents...

The books that let you escape into the wonderful world of romance! Trips to exotic places...interesting plots...meeting memorable people... the excitement of love....These are integral parts of Harlequin Presents— the heartwarming novels read by women everywhere.

Many early issues are now available. Choose from this great selection!

LILIAN PEAKE
the little impostor

ANNE MATHER
dangerous rhapsody

SARA CRAVEN
a gift for a lion

JANET DAILEY
bluegrass king

Choose from this great selection of exciting Harlequin Presents editions

Relive a great romance...
Harlequin Presents 1980
Complete and mail this coupon today!

Harlequin Reader Service

In U.S.A.
MPO Box 707
Niagara Falls, N.Y. 14302

In Canada
649 Ontario St.
Stratford, Ontario, N5A 6W2

Please send me the following Harlequin Presents novels. I am enclosing
my check or money order for $1.50 for each novel ordered, plus 59¢ to cover
postage and handling.

☐ 192	☐ 201	☐ 210
☐ 193	☐ 202	☐ 211
☐ 194	☐ 203	☐ 212
☐ 195	☐ 204	☐ 213
☐ 197	☐ 205	☐ 214
☐ 198	☐ 206	☐ 215
☐ 199	☐ 207	☐ 216
☐ 200	☐ 208	☐ 217

Number of novels checked @ $1.50 each = $_____

N.Y. State residents add appropriate sales tax $_____

Postage and handling $_____ .59

                                        TOTAL $_____

I enclose _____
(Please send check or money order. We cannot be responsible for cash sent
 through the mail.)

Prices subject to change without notice.

NAME _____
                        (Please Print)

ADDRESS _____

CITY _____

STATE/PROV. _____

ZIP/POSTAL CODE _____

Offer expires March 31, 1981   01256317•